JESSICA BECK

THE DONUT MYSTERIES, BOOK 36
PASTRY PENALTIES

The First Time Ever Published!

The 36th Donut Mystery.

Jessica Beck is the *New York Times* Bestselling Author of the Donut Mysteries, the Classic Diner Mysteries, the Ghost Cat Cozy Mysteries, and the Cast Iron Cooking Mysteries.

For the genuine Emily,
For being brave enough to follow her dreams

When Emily Hargraves's stuffed animals are kidnapped and ransomed, the police treat it as a joke, but when the apparent abductor ends up on the wrong end of a knife, things turn deadly serious in April Springs as Suzanne and Jake do their best to solve the murder before the killer has a chance to strike again.

CHAPTER 1

E VEN AT FIRST GLANCE, IT was obvious to the untrained
eye that the crime scene had been carefully staged.
After all, it wasn't every day that a stuffed animal
was found holding a murder weapon, with the victim lying just
a few paces away.

It was obviously someone's sick idea of a joke, but the body on
the bed was certainly no laughing matter.

As Spots held the knife loosely on top of his hoof, his two
best friends, Cow and Moose, looked on, and it didn't take a
great leap of imagination to believe that they were each aghast
by what they saw.

In some very real way, all three stuffed animals, much beloved
by the town of April Springs, North Carolina, were involved in
a murder that would end up shaking the town to its very core.

CHAPTER 2

Earlier That Day

"EMILY, ARE YOU OKAY?" I was working behind the counter of Donut Hearts when my friend walked in. The pretty young brunette looked as though she had just lost her best friend.

As a matter of fact, I was soon to learn that she'd lost three of them.

"Suzanne, I don't know what to do." Her voice had lost all hope and joy, which was really out of character for her.

"Tell me what's wrong. Was it Max? Did he hurt you?" Emily was engaged to my ex-husband, and I had to wonder if he hadn't pulled the same kind of boneheaded thing with her that he had done with me. I'd caught him cheating with a hairdresser when we'd been married. He could call the late Darlene Higgins a stylist all he wanted to, but she was a hairdresser who wore her skirts too tight and her blouses cut too low when she'd been alive, something that hadn't been lost on my husband's wandering eye.

"No. Max is an angel," she said absently.

I could agree to disagree on that particular point if I wanted to make a fuss about it, but I decided to let that one slide since Emily was clearly hurting. "Then what happened?"

Instead of answering my question directly, she thrust a handwritten note out to me. I took it, glanced at it, and then I called in back to my assistant. "Emma, I need you out front."

Emma Blake came at a trot, clearly happy to be working with me again. Her fine red hair was pulled back in a ponytail, and her freckles seemed to intensify more and more every day. Emma had taken a little time away from Donut Hearts to help her boyfriend, Barton Gleason, open a restaurant, and I'd worried that the temporary leave might become something more permanent, but she'd come back to me soon enough. When I'd asked her why, Emma had muttered something about being a little too close for comfort and about mixing business with pleasure, and I had left it at that, thrilled that she'd come back to the fold.

"Hey, Emily. What's going on?" She didn't even have to see the note to realize that something was wrong. "Did Max cheat on you?"

"Why does everyone keep asking me that?" Emily asked plaintively.

Emma looked at me and shrugged.

I chose not to respond to the question at all. "Can you give us a minute?" I asked Emma.

My assistant and Emily were best friends, and Emma looked a little puzzled by my request. Ordinarily, Emily would have come by the donut shop to see her, not me.

But clearly these weren't ordinary circumstances.

To her credit, Emma bounced back from the slight quickly. "Sure thing, Boss."

Emily nodded her thanks absently to Emma as I led her to a couch that was away from my other customers, at least for the moment. Foot traffic tended to ebb and flow during the last hour I was open for business, and if there was a pattern to my customers' coming and going, I hadn't been smart enough to recognize it yet.

Once we were both seated, I looked again at the paper she'd handed me.

IF YOU WANT TO SEE YOUR THREE BUDDYS AGAIN, PUT A HUNDRAD BUCKS IN THE TRASHCAN TONIGHT OUT BACK OR ELSE.

Spelling errors notwithstanding, it was clearly the act of a juvenile mind. "Three buddys" was obvious enough. It could refer only to Cow, Spots, and Moose, the three stuffed animals Emily's shop had been named for. They were much more than stuffed animals to her, though. Emily took great pride in displaying the three of them on a shelf of honor above the cash register, usually dressed in outlandish outfits, from togas to three-piece suits, Halloween costumes to Easter Bunny getups. They weren't just the namesakes for her shop; they were family to her. "Did you call the police?" I asked her.

"I tried. They just laughed at me."

I took a deep breath. "Are you telling me that Stephen Grant *laughed* at you?" I'd known our police chief since he'd been a rookie cop, and he was currently dating my best friend, Grace Gauge, but none of that would save him if I found out he wasn't taking Emily's problem seriously.

"No, I never got that far. They've got a new woman answering 9-1-1 calls, and the second I got this note and realized that the guys were missing, I phoned right away."

I grabbed my cell phone and dialed a number that was first in my queue. The moment my husband answered, I said, "Jake, I need you at the donut shop on the double."

"What's going on?" he asked me, the concern clear in his voice.

"Someone stole Cow, Spots, and Moose and left Emily a ransom note."

Jake paused for a moment before answering, and I could just imagine my former state police investigator husband trying to figure out if I was pulling his leg or not. I decided to put that worry out of his mind. "This is the real deal, Jake. Emily is barely hanging on."

That got his attention. I know just how much my husband loves me, but that doesn't mean he can't light up when an attractive young woman smiles at him, and Emily was a particular favorite of his. "I'm on my way," he said.

"Thanks."

I hung up and saw Emily looking expectantly at me. "Is he coming?"

"He is on his way even as we speak," I assured her, being careful not to touch the note any more than I had to. I doubted this criminal mastermind had his prints on file with the FBI, but why muddy the waters if I didn't have to? "Don't worry. He'll get to the bottom of this."

Emily frowned for a moment, and I could see her façade start to crack a little more. "You probably think I'm being silly, but I can't help it. Those three guys mean the world to me."

"I get it, Emily. You don't have to explain it to me," I said, patting her shoulder. "You grew up with them."

"The truth is, they were the only friends I had for a long time," she said softly.

I couldn't imagine sweet Emily having any trouble making friends, but then again, I knew how hard it could be to make new pals. She'd embraced their presence so wholeheartedly that when I heard her talking to the three stuffed animals, I swore that I often expected them to answer!

"Don't worry. Jake will find them."

"I hope so. I really hope so," she said as Jake appeared. We lived close to the shop, but he must have cut across the park at a dead trot to get there so quickly. I wasn't even sure he could have driven there that fast. Tall and thin, Jake's stride was tough for me to keep up with on my best day.

He ran his hand over his short blond hair before he spoke.

Jessica Beck

"How are you doing?" he asked Emily as he slid onto the couch between us.

"I'm losing my mind with worry," she said, her voice shaking a little as she spoke.

"Let me see the note," he said, his voice full of calm authority.

"I've got it right here," I said as I handed it to him by the edges.

Jake pulled out a clear plastic evidence bag and carefully sealed the note inside. It didn't surprise me that he had a clear bag with him, since he took them everywhere he went, just in case.

My husband studied the block letters and the word choices before looking at her carefully. "Who under the age of eighteen has a grudge against you?" he asked her.

"You know, it could be an adult," I said.

Jake frowned at me before turning back to Emily. "That's true, but I think we'd be safe to assume that we're dealing with a juvenile until we learn differently."

"It has to be Charlie Jefferson," Emily said after a moment's thought. "I caught him shoplifting last week, and I called the police. It was the third time I saw him trying to steal something, and I warned him what would happen if he kept it up. How did he get into the newsstand, though? I'm so careful about locking up the shop every night."

"Let's find Charlie and ask him," Jake said as he stood up.

"All three of us?" I asked, eager to be invited. I loved seeing Jake work, even if it was just cracking an easy case like this appeared to be.

"It's fine with me, but ultimately it's up to Emily," Jake said with a shrug.

"Please come with us, Suzanne, if you can get away from the shop."

"Just give me a second with Emma," I replied. I approached

6

my assistant, who was cleaning the counter in front of her with more focus than she normally used. There wasn't a doubt in my mind that she'd been eavesdropping on our conversation. I couldn't really blame her. If our roles had been reversed, I'd have been doing the same thing myself. "Can you hold down the fort for a while?" I asked her.

"Of course. Is she okay?" Emma asked as she glanced furtively at Emily.

"She's not at the moment, but I'm sure she'll soon be. Don't worry. Emily's in good hands. I'm sure she'll tell you all about it as soon as it's over."

"If she doesn't, I expect you to," Emma said.

"If I can. If I don't make it back by closing, you know the drill."

"Yes, ma'am," she said with a salute. With a more serious face, she added, "Suzanne, take good care of her, would you?"

"I'll do my best," I said.

I found Jake and Emily already outside. "Ready?" I asked them.

"Sure, but we need a ride," Jake said. "I hurried over here on foot, and Emily didn't drive, either."

"The Jeep it is, then," I said as I led them to my vehicle. Jake took the back seat, over Emily's protestations. "Where do you suggest we start looking for Charlie?"

"Unless I miss my guess, he's in school right now," Jake said.

"Ordinarily you'd be right, but I'm betting he's out running around town somewhere. Then again, he might even be at home," I said.

"How could you possibly know that?" Jake asked me.

"I've had several kids coming into Donut Hearts this morning," I said. "It's supposedly some kind of a half teachers' workday or something like that."

"Only half the teachers get off, too?" Emily asked.

"No, I meant they only work half a day," I said.

"Oh," she said, clearly distracted by her lost companions. "Do you think they are okay?" she asked Jake as she turned in her seat.

"They're fine. Charlie isn't going to touch them until he gets his money," Jake said with calm self-assurance.

"I hope you're right," Emily said.

Since no one made any suggestions as to where we should start looking for Charlie, I headed to the edge of town.

Jake tapped my shoulder. "Don't tell me you know where this kid lives."

"I've been here all my life," I said. "As a matter of fact, his mother, Jasmine, and I went to high school together. She's living in her parents' old house."

"Wow, why did you even need me?" Jake asked a little lightheartedly.

"For more reasons than I can even begin to list," I said with a grin.

We pulled up in front of Jasmine's house five minutes later. After all, April Springs wasn't really all that big. It was a cottage not much bigger than the one I lived in with Jake, but that was where the similarity ended. Our place was freshly painted and in good repair, our yard was neat and tidy. This house could have been the "before" picture in a dramatic house makeover show on television. Parts of the guttering hung down, while other sections sported a growing forest of weeds and trees. Weathered and broken shingles covered most of the roof, while three blue tarps covered other sections. The porch railing in front was hit or miss, and there was a washing machine on the front porch and a broken-down old truck in the yard that would clearly never run again.

"Wow, how can anyone live like this?" Emily asked.

"I doubt that I could," I said as we got out and started up the broken concrete sidewalk to the front door.

"Doubt? You just doubt? Does that mean that you're not sure?" Jake asked. "You couldn't stand it, and you know it."

"You couldn't, either," I retorted.

"That's true enough." When we reached the front door, he turned to us and said, "Ladies, let me do the talking. I know how to handle situations like this."

"Jake, we aren't raiding a crack den. It's just a kid," I reminded him.

"Kids can be dangerous, too, and don't forget it," he said.

"You're armed, aren't you?" I asked, knowing that as much as I hated to admit it, he was right. Craziness wasn't just limited to adults, especially these days.

He gestured down to his ankle holster. "We're good to go." Jake knocked on the front door, and I worried that it wouldn't be able to stand up to his summons. It wasn't that he was pounding that hard. It was just that the door, like the rest of the house, had seen better days.

No one answered.

"What should we do?" Emily asked.

Jake replied by knocking again.

There was still no response.

"Is there a chance he's in there and just won't come to the door?" I asked softly. If I were in his position, I wasn't sure that I'd answer our summons, either.

"Of course there is," Jake said softly. In a loud voice full of authority, he said, "Charlie, you need to come to the door immediately. You have six seconds."

I whispered to my husband, "What are we doing if he doesn't make your deadline?"

"There's not much chance of that happening. If he's in there, he'll come out," Jake said confidently.

Six seconds passed, then twelve, and finally, a full minute.

Jake frowned at the door, and then he reached out a hand and tried the doorknob.

It turned easily in his hand.

"Isn't this breaking and entering?" Emily asked him.

"Did you see me break anything?" Jake asked with a slight grin. "I haven't taken a single step inside, so I'm not even entering."

"You know what she means," I said.

"It might come under the heading unlawful entry," Jake corrected us as he looked around, being careful not to violate the threshold. He might not have been a cop anymore, but he still abided by the rules that had driven his professional life all those years. "Hello? Is anyone home?" he called out.

Again, there was no response. The place, at least what I could see of it, was just as bad as the exterior had been. The furniture was worn out, and there were several trash bags overflowing with debris filled with the evidence of a thousand poor choices.

Emily started to go in when Jake reached out and put a hand on her shoulder. "Hold on."

"What if my stuffed animals are inside? I have to see," she said.

"Not this way," Jake replied.

"What should we do, then? The police think this is just one big joke."

"Still, we do it by the book," Jake said. "Let's walk around the house and check the windows. Maybe we can see something inside that gives us cause to enter."

If it had just been Emily and me, I would have plowed right inside behind her, but I knew that crossing Jake wasn't an option. After all, I'd been the one to call him in on the case. I couldn't very well ignore him the moment it got a little inconvenient for me. "Lead on," I said.

The three of us walked around the house, but it didn't do us much good. Most of the windows were covered with sheets and towels or such a thick layer of grime that seeing inside was nearly impossible anyway.

"Can I help you with something?" someone called out behind us.

I saw Jake crouch as his hand went to his ankle in an instant. Wow. I hadn't realized just how fast his reactions were.

The three of us turned and saw a woman in her seventies wearing a tattered housecoat, soiled slippers, and old-fashioned curlers in her hair.

Jake stood again, without his weapon, and I found myself letting out my breath. Funny, but I hadn't even realized that I'd been holding it.

"We're looking for Jasmine and Charlie," I said, putting on my brightest smile.

"You just missed them." The old lady cackled before adding, "Four days ago. They went to live with her brother somewhere in Texas. Good riddance, I say." The woman sized us up for a moment before adding with a crooked smile, "The place just happens to be for rent. I can give you a fair price if you want it right now."

"Thanks, but we're good," I said. I wouldn't have lived there on a dare, let alone paid for the privilege.

Her fleeting smile was gone as quickly as it had arrived. "Then I'd appreciate it if you'd move on. After all, you can't be too careful these days," she added.

"No, ma'am. You can't," I said.

"What now?" Emily asked once we were back in the Jeep. "If they've been gone that long, Charlie couldn't have left the ransom note, let alone stolen the guys from me in the first place."

"We just keep digging," Jake said. "Don't worry. We're not going to give up until your friends are safely back with you."

Her smile of thanks was enough to warm the oldest curmudgeon's heart, and my husband was certainly touched by it. "I don't know how to even begin to thank you."

"Where's Max, by the way?" I asked her as I started the Jeep. I'd been surprised that my ex-husband hadn't dropped everything to be with his fiancée in her time of need.

"He's shooting a commercial in LA," Emily said.

"Good for him," I said. I'd been under the impression that Max's commercial work had dried up lately. "What's he selling this time?"

Emily shrugged. "He wouldn't tell me. All he would say was that it would be shown only in Japan."

It must have been for a truly embarrassing product if he wouldn't even tell Emily. I'd have to wheedle it out of him at some point, but for now, we had a more important task at hand.

The only problem was that we had no idea where to look.

CHAPTER 3

As I drove us back to town, Jake said, "You know, there's something odd about this note."

I glanced in the rearview mirror and saw him studying the ransom note, still safely ensconced in its plastic bag.

"Do you mean *besides* the spelling errors and the messy block letters?" I asked him.

"That's the thing. I'm not absolutely certain we should be looking for a juvenile after all."

"Do you honestly think that an adult could write something that badly?" Emily asked.

"They might if they were trying to throw us off their trail," Jake said. "Emily, the entire town knows how much you love Cow, Spots, and Moose. If someone wanted to hurt you, what better way to do it than to steal them from you?"

"That's true enough," Emily said. "But if that's the case, why not just take them and not bother leaving a ransom note behind?"

She had a valid point, but I wasn't about to say anything. Was Jake making more of this than there was, just for something constructive to do? I'd once had a boyfriend in high school whose car had a headlight out. Instead of doing the logical thing, which was replacing the light, he'd checked the wiring from the battery to the light terminals. Only after two hours of mucking about did he take my suggestion to actually try the headlight itself. Needless to say, we didn't last long after that.

Some folks just didn't like having the obvious pointed out to them.

"Maybe whoever did it just *wants* you to think that a kid did it," Jake said.

"What exactly are you basing that assumption on?" I asked him as delicately as I could.

"Pull over and I'll show you," he said.

I was getting close to the grocery store, so I did as he suggested and found an empty spot in the parking lot. As I shut the engine off, Jake handed the note forward. "Look at it closely and tell me what you see," he told me as Emily looked on as well.

"I see a poorly written note asking for ransom money," I said dismissively as I started to hand it back to him.

"Look at the quality of the lines, Suzanne," he insisted.

I did as he asked and peered at the note a little closer. I hadn't really noticed it before, but the lines used to print the block letters were strong and firm, neat and crisp, as opposed to the message the letters conveyed. "It was done with a firm, sure hand," I said.

"Good. Now ask yourself something. Would a teenager committing theft and extortion have a firm, sure hand while writing a ransom note asking for money?" he asked me.

A shadow of doubt began to creep into my mind. "No, probably not."

Jake looked pleased by my conclusion.

"But what does that mean?" Emily asked.

"I think an adult wanted to throw you off their scent," Jake said.

"Why ask for a hundred dollars, then?" she wanted to know.

"It's to give the note some verisimilitude," Jake said. "You can put the money in the trash as you've been asked, but I seriously doubt anyone is going to pick it up."

"I still have to try," Emily said plaintively.

"I understand that, but in the meantime, are there any adults you've crossed lately or had any conflicts with?"

Emily frowned a moment before speaking. "It's hard to say. I'm not exactly living a life that promotes confrontation on a daily basis," she said.

"Think hard, Emily. It's important," I said.

"Let me think about it. I suppose if I had to, I could make you a list. There may be a name or two that might belong on it."

"Start thinking about it," Jake said. "Now, how about Max?"

"What's Max got to do with this?" I asked, wondering why my current husband was talking about his predecessor.

"Think about it, Suzanne. What does Max care about more than anything in the world?"

"*Besides* Max, you mean?" I asked him.

"Yes, besides himself," he answered.

"Emily," I said without a moment's hesitation.

"Emily what?" she asked upon hearing her name. She'd been so intent on going through a list of acquaintances in her mind who might be holding a grudge that clearly she hadn't been paying any attention to our conversation.

"You're the most important thing in Max's life," I stated simply and plainly.

"He cared for you too, once upon a time," Emily said, clearly trying to mollify me.

"Please, we're both long past that. Jake's point is that if someone wanted to get back at Max, they'd most likely come after you. Can you think of anyone your fiancé has had words with lately?"

Emily shrugged before speaking. "You know Max. He has a tendency to be overly dramatic at times. Some folks around here don't know how to take him."

"You need to make a separate list of those folks you know of, too," Jake suggested.

Emily looked uncomfortable by the request. "Really? Is that completely necessary?"

"You want to get your pals back, right?" I asked her.

"You know I do," she said. "I'll keep thinking about both lists."

"Good," Jake said from the backseat. "I'm assuming the newsstand is closed right now."

"No, my mother is running it for me while I'm gone," she said.

"Would it be all right for us to go over there?" he asked her.

"Of course it is. After all, it's my shop. What do you hope to find?"

"I'd like to look for evidence of a break-in, or the lack of one," he said.

"What does that mean?" Emily asked.

I could answer that one for her myself. "If someone had a key, or some other access that wouldn't require breaking into the store, that would present a very different list of suspects than if the lock was forced open."

I looked back at Jake for confirmation, and he nodded at me as he winked. I felt like the teacher's star pupil. While I considered myself a master donut maker, my sleuthing was purely done on an amateur basis, so kudos from a seasoned pro were always greatly appreciated.

"Then let's go have a look," Emily said.

"I have a question for you. Who else has a key to the shop?" I asked her as I drove toward Two Cows and a Moose.

"Nobody," she said.

"Nobody? Not even your mother?" Jake asked her.

"Well, of course *she* has one," Emily said.

"So that makes two. Doesn't Jenny Barnes come in and restock sometimes for you when you're closed?" I asked. Jenny was a friend of Emma's, and I'd heard them talking about it one day not that long ago.

"Yes, of course. How else could she get in? She's paying her way through college working half a dozen part-time jobs. I don't pay her much, I can't afford to, but she's a sweet girl."

"Now we're at three. Is there anyone else? Do you have a cleaning crew?" I asked her.

"No. Of course not. I couldn't afford that."

I had a sudden thought. "Emily, when you were flooded out and had to relocate to my storefront, did you give out any keys to the workmen?"

She nodded, a look of dread crossing her face. "I must have had a dozen keys made for all of the workers who had to come in and out."

Her face clouded up even further as Jake followed up with the logical question we were surely all thinking. "Did you happen to think to change the locks when you reopened the shop?"

"It never even crossed my mind," Emily said, clearly about to explode in tears. "It's my fault, isn't it? *I'm* the reason it was so easy for someone to kidnap the guys."

I touched her shoulder lightly. "Don't think of it that way," I said. "How could you possibly know any of this was going to happen?"

"I should have been smarter about it," she said, getting her emotions under control.

"I'd have those locks changed this afternoon if I were you," Jake said.

"What good would that do now? It's kind of like locking the barn door after the horses escape, isn't it?" she asked.

"Regardless of what happens with your friends, you don't want your shop to be vulnerable like that," he said.

"Yes, you're right. I'll make a call once we get inside."

We were out in front of the newsstand, and I parked my Jeep

away from the front door, an old habit I'd gotten into running the donut shop. The prime spots were for paying customers. I couldn't even break the pattern when I was one of those very same customers myself.

As we walked inside, I couldn't help but glance up at the shelf where the three stuffed animals usually reigned over the newsstand.

Their absence threw the universe out of whack for me.

I could only imagine how Emily must be feeling.

We needed to get those three back in their rightful place, no matter how silly the police might think the task sounded.

I hadn't noticed what my husband had been up to, but the moment we walked in, he went straight for both door locks and examined them carefully. It took him only a minute for the both of them, and he shook his head as he looked at me.

"Does that mean that someone broke in, or they didn't?" I asked him as I approached.

"There are no signs of tampering. I'm not saying that an excellent lock picker couldn't have gotten in, but considering the crime, I think we'll have to just assume that whoever stole the stuffed animals had a key to the place."

"Which doesn't really do us much good, does it?" I asked him softly. I looked up to see Emily talking with her mother, Christine, a once-plump woman, now as slender as her daughter, blessed with an excellent fashion sense. Her clothes always seemed to fit her perfectly, and I wondered about the size of her clothing budget. Chances were very good that it far exceeded mine, but that wouldn't have taken much.

After conferring a few moments, the mother and daughter approached us together. Since Christine had lost so much weight, she and Emily were beginning to look more like sisters than anything else. Christine spoke first. "I wasn't sure I should say anything to you, but Emily insists. The truth of the matter is that I was sure it was just a crank call."

"What happened?" I asked her before Jake could beat me to it.

"Someone called here two minutes before you walked in and said, 'Tell them they're cold, and getting colder.' When I asked what in the world they were talking about, the voice just said, 'Don't worry about it. They'll know,' and then they hung up. Does that mean anything to you?"

"Someone picked the wrong people to challenge," Jake said, obviously irritated that we'd been followed, and worse yet, he hadn't spotted the tail. I was angry as well. It was bad enough stealing Emily's stuffed animals, but now they were openly mocking us in our efforts to retrieve them. I realized that Jake had been right. We were clearly dealing with someone more than just a disgruntled teenager. "Did you get any sense of who might be calling, Christine?" Jake asked her.

"No. The voice was so soft that I couldn't even tell if it was a man or a woman," she explained.

"Were there any distinguishing background noises?" I asked.

Jake nodded in approval, even as Christine shook her head. "I had two customers in the shop at the time, so I didn't really get a chance to pick up on anything nuanced. I'm sorry, but I honestly thought it was a crank call until Emily spoke up."

"It's fine," I told Christine. "I'm glad you told us. Did anything else odd happen while your daughter was gone?"

"Well, four different shoppers commented on the absence of our mascots," she said, and Emily cringed a little. Christine touched her daughter's shoulder lightly. "It's okay, dear. I'm sure you'll find them."

"We just have to," Emily said.

"Do you want to write down the names you've been

considering for you and Max?" I asked her gently. "After all, your lists are the best place for us to start looking."

"What kind of lists are you making, Emily?" Christine asked.

"Suzanne and Jake think that whoever took the guys might have a grudge against Max or me," she explained.

"Surely no adult would do something so juvenile," she said.

"We think it might be someone trying to make it *look* as though a kid did it," I told her.

"Why on earth would anyone do that?" Christine asked pointedly. "That just doesn't make any sense to me."

"Stealing three stuffed animals and trying to get a ransom payment for their safe return doesn't make a great deal of sense either," I said, "and yet it happened."

"What does Max have to do with this?" Christine asked a little pointedly. I got the distinct impression that the future mother-in-law wasn't all that thrilled about her daughter's choice in men, but she was doing a good job hiding it from her daughter.

"Probably nothing, Mom," Emily said, quickly killing the topic of her betrothed. "I'm sure whoever did this was coming after me."

"My dear sweet child, who in the world could possibly have a grudge against *you*?" Christine asked with a smile.

"You'd be surprised," Emily said, and then she turned to us. "Give me a second and I'll write up both of those lists for you."

Emily walked over to the register and got out a pad and a pen. As she jotted down a few names, Christine touched my arm and pulled me aside. "Suzanne, may I speak with you for a moment?"

"Of course," I said.

"Alone?" she asked as she glanced over at Jake.

"Christine, anything you have to say to me, you can say in front of my husband."

"This isn't about the stuffed animals, dear. It's personal."

I was about to protest again when Jake said, "Ladies, if you'll excuse me, I want to take another look at those locks before we go."

It was clearly just a way to give Christine what she'd requested. I didn't mind Jake leaving. Anything Christine said to me would be repeated to my husband at the first opportunity.

"What is this about?" I asked her once Jake was gone, not that I didn't have my suspicions.

"Are you at all concerned about Emily marrying your ex-husband?" she asked, the words coming out in a near whisper. I had a feeling that she didn't want her daughter overhearing this particular conversation.

"Actually, I'm not. Max is in love with Emily in a way that he never managed to achieve with me," I answered. "She's changed him in ways I frankly didn't think were possible."

"Then you approve?" she asked, clearly taken aback by what I'd just told her. "You two *are* friends, aren't you?"

"Me and Emily, or me and Max?" I asked. "Never mind, it's the same answer either way. Yes, I'm friends with both of them."

"Even after he cheated on you? How is that possible?" she asked, clearly worried about Emily's heart and her daughter's future well-being.

"The Max who did that to me is not the same man who wants to marry your daughter," I said. "Do you believe that people can change, Christine?"

"I think it's possible, but I'm not all that sure that it happens very often in real life," she admitted.

"I can't fault the logic of that argument, but in my opinion, Max is one of the rare ones who has managed to do it," I said.

"Do you truly believe that?"

"I do," I said, oddly mimicking the words I'd spoken at the altar once upon a time with the man in question.

"I hope you are right," she said, clearly still fretting over her daughter's choice in men.

"I am sure of it, but even if I'm wrong, your daughter is crazy about the man, so there's really nothing anyone can do about it," I reminded her gently. "Christine, you need to trust Emily's judgment."

"Even if she's wrong? What do I do if it all falls apart?" she asked. The woman appeared to be on the verge of some kind of breakdown, and I couldn't help but feel bad for her.

"Then you will be there to help her pick up the pieces if something bad happens. What else can you do? My momma was there when it happened to me, and I know that you'll be there for Emily if you need to be."

"Your mother is an extraordinary woman," Christine said.

"As are you," I answered warmly.

Christine surprised me by hugging me just as Emily walked up. "What's going on, you two?"

"I was just thanking Suzanne for looking for your three little friends," Christine said, doing her best to wipe her tears away out of her daughter's line of vision.

"It's already been taken care of. I've thanked them both half a dozen times already myself," Emily told her mother.

"Still, one more won't hurt," she said. "Now, if you'll excuse me, I really must see to cleaning the floor near the comic books."

"They're called graphic novels, Mom," Emily said with a smile.

"Call them whatever you'd like, but someone spilled popcorn on the floor, and it's been driving me crazy. We don't even sell popcorn!"

"One of the mysteries of life, I suppose," Emily said, looking at her mother with great fondness. The two women clearly had a special bond. Emily and I shared that in common as well. Each of our mothers were also our good friends, something that still amazed me. "Here's the list, Suzanne."

She handed me a piece of paper neatly divided into two sections. One said "MAX," while the other one was headed "EMILY." Max's list had two names on it, and Emily's had only one. The ratio didn't surprise me one bit. In all honesty, I had expected Max's list to have even more entries than that. "I'm still not certain why I had to write these names down, since I'm going with you when you talk to these people," she added.

"About that," I said. "Emily, it might be better if you stay here, just in case there is another call."

"Suzanne Hart, you're not going to get rid of me that easily. I want to be there when you find my friends. They need to see me."

Emily was slipping back into the habit of referring to her three stuffed animals as sentient beings, something that was devilishly easy to do myself when I was around her.

I was searching for a way to address my concerns when Jake joined us. "Actually, having you with us might hurt the investigation," he said.

I thought the same thing, but I certainly wasn't going to be so blunt stating it.

I was about to backpedal a little for Jake when Emily asked us, "Are you telling me that I could actually make things worse? Is that true?"

"Emily, the thing is, people might not feel as free to talk with you there," I said softly. "You understand, don't you?"

"Not really, but I don't want to make things harder than they have to be if I can help it," she conceded.

"Can you tell us why these names are on the lists you made?" Jake asked her. It was an excellent question, and I chided myself for not thinking of asking it myself. "All we need are the highlights. We'll dig into the rest."

"I can do that. In a nutshell, Dusty and I have a history, or so he wishes. We had a rather unpleasant encounter yesterday, and I could easily see him doing something this petty to get back at me."

"How about the other names? The ones that made Max's list?" I asked.

"Hattie Moon is furious that Max wouldn't cast her for some silly part in his play, and she's been complaining all over town about him for days. In fact, she threatened to burn the place down if she didn't get her way! As for Michelle Pennington, she has a crush on Max. She's had one for years, but lately she's been trying to win him back in the most obvious ways, and he keeps rebuffing her. The odd thing is, I know for a fact that she's been dating Dusty all the while. What can you expect from small-town living? Sometimes it feels as though *all* of our lives are intertwined. Do you need anything more?"

"No, you've told us everything we need to know to get started," Jake said.

Christine broke things up by calling out, "Emily, is there a receptacle anywhere near here? If there is, it must be covered in books."

"Hang on a second. I'm coming, Mom," she said, but before she left us, she said, "Find them. Please. I'm begging you."

"We're going to do our best," I said.

Jake touched my arm. "Suzanne, let's get going."

"Call me as soon as you learn anything," Emily said. "Promise me you'll do that. And be careful around Dusty. He's not as harmless as he looks."

"We'll do just that," I said.

Jake headed for the door, and I followed suit. As I neared the door, I glanced back at Christine. Our gazes met, and she gave me a look that said a thousand things without verbalizing a word.

24

I nodded back in response, trying to put as much into it as I could, and then I joined Jake outside at the Jeep.

It was time to continue with our investigation and see what we could learn about the missing store mascots.

CHAPTER 4

"CAN YOU TELL ME ANYTHING more about the people we're going to be speaking with this afternoon?" Jake asked once we were back in the Jeep, alone this time.

Before I started the engine, I handed both lists to him. "I think Emily did a pretty good job of summing things up. I hadn't realized that Michelle was seeing Dusty, but then again, contrary to popular belief, I don't know *everything* that goes on in April Springs."

"Funny, but I thought that Max would have more than two names on his list. If you ask me, *he's* the reason behind all of this," my husband said with the hint of a frown.

"Why, because he's my ex?" I asked him. My husband had never really warmed up to his predecessor, which made perfect sense to me.

"No, because he's an idiot," Jake said rather bluntly.

"I wouldn't call him that on his worst day," I said, being in the unusual position of defending Max yet again, this time to Jake. "You don't really know him all that well."

"Suzanne, he let *you* go, so really, that's *all* I need to know about him."

I touched his arm lightly and smiled. "It's sweet of you to say so."

"Not that I'm complaining," Jake said, matching my grin with one of his own. "If he hadn't been so monumentally stupid as to cheat on you, I wouldn't be with you now. Where should we start?"

"Michelle Pennington is the first name she wrote down for Max," I said. "Why don't we start with her?"

"I've never even heard of the woman. How well do you know her?"

"Not all that well at all, but I suppose I'd have to say a little bit, anyway."

"From the donut shop?" Jake asked as I started driving. I knew where Michelle worked, so at least that made tracking her down easy enough.

"Donuts? Michelle? No way. She thinks they are poison."

"If they are, then they are tasty, tasty poison," Jake replied. "What's her problem, anyway? What does she have against donuts?"

"It's not just the treats I sell," I said. "Michelle doesn't approve of sugar in any form whatsoever. The woman is fanatical about what she eats, or at least she used to be. Honestly, I haven't seen her in a while. We don't exactly run in the same circles."

"What does she do for a living?"

"The last I heard, she was working for an accounting firm in a strip mall on the way toward Maple Hollow," I said. As we drove by the hardware store, the newspaper, and the bank, I wondered why Michelle would be on Max's most recent list of enemies. I knew that they'd dated just before he'd started seeing Emily, but from what I remembered, it had flamed out rather spectacularly. She was at least ten years younger than my ex, and though he tried his best, he couldn't keep up with her in the end, so he ended things with her, or so he claimed. From what I'd gathered, Michelle hadn't been particularly happy about the split.

"Max doesn't seem like the type to date an accountant," Jake said.

"She's not an accountant; she's the receptionist," I said.

"Okay. That I can see."

"Jake, from what I know about Michelle, she's smarter than you might think. If she's working as a receptionist, it's because that's what she *chooses* to do at this point in her life, not that there's anything wrong with her job. Hey, I make donuts for a living, so who am I to judge? In many ways, her job is a lot better than mine is. I guess what I'm trying to say is that Max has good taste in women," I explained carefully to him.

"Because he married you. I certainly agree with that."

"And he's with Emily now, too," I reminded him. "You're a fan of hers, and don't even bother trying to deny it."

"I wouldn't dream of it." Jake frowned for a moment as we pulled up in front of the accounting office, which was located between a chiropractor and a frozen-yogurt place. "What I *don't* understand is why do so many quality women go out with duds? Are you all trying to reform the bad boys, or is there some kind of charm to him in particular that I'm not getting?"

"Well, he's certainly handsome," I said, and before I could finish the thought, Jake interrupted.

"Please. I know you better than that, Suzanne. There's got to be more to it than that."

"What you asked me earlier is true enough. Max has a way of charming you without you realizing that it's even happening. It's hard to explain, but when that man is giving you his attention, it's complete and undivided. It feels as though there is nothing more important in the world than you are to him at that moment. It's honestly a little intoxicating."

"I suppose it would have to be," Jake said as he nodded. "I'm just glad that you were able to break yourself away from his sway."

"Seeing him with Darlene made that easy enough," I said. I leaned over and kissed my husband before I got out of the car. "The truth is that I was devastated at the time, but I'm glad it happened. If he hadn't cheated on me, I wouldn't be with you right now."

"At least we can agree on that," Jake said with a smile. Was it possible that my current husband was a little jealous of his predecessor? I'd have to do everything in my power to reassure him that I had no, and I mean zero, interest in Max, at least not romantically.

"So, how do we tackle this?" Jake asked me as we neared the door.

"I've got a thought. Will you play along with me?"

He shrugged. "Your ideas are pretty solid. Sure, why not?"

"I appreciate the confidence," I said as I opened the door. "Lead on."

Michelle hadn't changed a bit since I'd last seen her. She was the fittest woman I'd ever known in my life. Maybe giving up donuts, and all of their sweet siblings, wasn't such a bad idea after all, especially if I could look like she did. Then again, Jake liked me kind of curvy, and who was I to try to convince him that he was wrong? I wasn't surprised to see that Michelle had a pashmina draped across her shoulders, even though the office wasn't all that cool. The woman was quite stylish, and she was always accessorizing with some kind of wrap or another, and her dangling jewelry looked to be a health hazard to me.

"Hello, Suzanne," she said curtly to me the moment she saw me walk in. Her taciturn look eased somewhat when she spotted Jake just behind me. After Michelle made a show of getting up from the desk and walking straight to my husband, she extended a hand as she also offered him a smile that offered a great deal more than just a warm welcome. If Jake noticed her focused attention, he didn't react to it. "You must be Jake Bishop. I understand that you are a state police investigator."

"I used to be," he said as he took her hand briefly before releasing it again, her jewelry jangling a little as she dropped her arm in surprise.

Michelle frowned for just a moment, clearly surprised that her charm hadn't instantly won him over. Wow, this woman's ego had done nothing but grow since the last time I'd seen her.

She turned her attention back to me when she saw that Jake was impervious to her charisma. "What can I do for you?"

"We're here about the key to the newsstand," I said.

Jake's right eyebrow arched slightly at the statement, but that was nothing compared to Michelle's reaction. "Key? What key? I don't have a key."

I looked at the list Emily had given me and pretended to study it. "Are you certain about that? Your name is on my list."

"Let me see that," she said as she made a grab for the document.

I couldn't very well allow that. As I pulled it back toward my chest, I said, "I'm sorry, but I'm not allowed to show this to anyone. Why would your name be on the list if you didn't have a key?" I tried to make the query sound more like an accusation than a question.

"I'm sure I have no idea," she said.

This wasn't working as well as I'd hoped. Was it time to concede that my gamble had been nothing but a bluff, or should I double down and go all in? Jake had taught me that in poker parlance, that meant sticking to my lie and pushing even harder, even when things began to look bleak. His expression was much more elegant than anything that I could have come up with.

"Think hard, Ms. Pennington," Jake said beside me. It was clear enough that he was ready to commit as well, and I loved him even more for it.

Michelle pretended to ponder it for a few moments before she finally said, "You're talking about Arnie's key, aren't you?"

"Arnie?" I asked.

"Arnie White. He and I were dating when the newsstand flooded, and Arnie helped replumb the shop. It was *his* key, not mine. I don't believe that I ever even saw it."

We would need to speak with Arnie White to see if that were indeed true, but in the meantime, it was time to press her a little harder on the real reason for our visit. "I understand you and Max had a fight recently." I didn't happen to have that specific bit of information, but it was a fair gamble. Otherwise why would Emily have written her name down on Max's list?

She frowned openly at this. "I'm not sure what business that is of yours. After all, he divorced you years ago."

"*She* divorced *him*," Jake reminded her.

Michelle waved a hand in the air. "Whatever. It's *all* ancient history. Max and I are through. I moved on weeks ago. Does it even matter? Why do you care, Suzanne?"

"Emily's stuffed animals are missing," I said, watching her gaze.

She didn't flinch upon hearing the news, but that really didn't necessarily mean anything. "So?"

"So, do you know anything about it?" I asked her.

Michelle shook her head. "What a ridiculous question," she said. "Of course not."

"Have you been here all day?" Jake asked her. It was an excellent point of inquiry, given the telephone call Christine had gotten at the newsstand earlier. Whoever had kidnapped the three guys had followed us out to the Jefferson place. I had chosen my partner well, for a great many reasons.

"We open at ten," she said curtly.

"And you've been here since then?" I asked her. "If I ask one of your bosses, will they confirm that?"

I'd started to head for one of the closed doors when Michelle stepped in front of me. "You can't just barge in there and start asking them questions."

"Can't we?" I asked. I stepped around her, wondering if she'd have the guts to try to stop me physically, but I never found out.

"Fine," she conceded before I had to carry out my bluff. "I had an appointment this morning, so I just got into the office ten minutes ago. What could it possibly matter to you?"

"Someone has been following us around town this morning while we investigate," Jake said.

"My, don't the two of you have high opinions of yourselves?" she asked him. "I'm sure you're just imagining it."

"Michelle, did you take Cow, Spots, and Moose to get back at Max?" I asked her point-blank. It had been one thing to mention the theft of the stuffed animals, but I wanted to confront her directly with the question.

Michelle looked clearly taken off guard by the directness of my inquiry. After taking a moment to collect herself, she asked me, "Do you honestly think that I would stoop to stealing Emily's stuffed animals? How childish do you think I am? Did she tell you that I took them? What is wrong with that woman? She got Max. She won, so why won't she leave me out of her drama?"

Ignoring the barrage of questions, I proposed a theory. "It would be a great way of getting back at Max after your recent argument."

"I wouldn't have touched Emily's prized possessions on a bet. Besides, I never had a key, so how am I supposed to have gotten in? Go on. Ask Arnie. He'll back me up on that."

"Oh, we will," I said.

That seemed to trouble her a little more than it should have. "Are you seriously giving me all of this grief because a few stuffed animals were stolen?"

"Three, not a few, and yes, that's exactly what we're doing."

"I think it's time for you both to leave," she said as she took a step toward the door. "This is where the insanity needs to end."

I wasn't about to budge, but then one of the doors opened, and an older gentleman with a magnificent head of gray hair stepped out. He was smoothing out an imaginary crease in his suit lapel when he spotted us. "Suzanne? How are you? How is your mother?"

"She's fine, sir," I said. I hadn't remembered that Harvey Bascomb was friends with Momma. "Harvey, this is my husband, Jake Bishop."

Harvey shook Jake's hand. "Glad to meet you." And then he turned back to me. "I'm glad to hear that your mother is well." He then turned to Michelle and asked, "Is everything all right here?"

I could have stuck it to her just then, but it wouldn't have been fair, especially if she was as innocent as she claimed. I decided to answer the question for her. "We just stopped by to ask her if she wanted to buy a raffle ticket."

"What's the raffle for?" he asked. "I'm always good for a worthy cause."

I patted my pockets, looking for tickets that didn't exist. "Oh, dear. I must have left them in the donut shop. We'll come back later."

As we hurried for the door, he called out, "See that you do. I'm good for at least one."

Michelle shot me a look that combined relief and confusion as we walked out, which was fine with me. I'd found that over the years, it was always best to leave my suspects wondering just what I was up to, even if I didn't always know the answer to that question myself.

"Raffle?" Jake asked me once we were outside. "What raffle?"

"What can I say? It was the first thing that popped into my head," I said.

"Suzanne, do we need to start a raffle now so we can sell Mr. Bascomb a ticket?"

"No worries. He'll probably forget about it," I said. "What do you think of Michelle's story?" I asked as I started the Jeep and drove out of the parking lot.

"I'd say she definitely had a fight with Max recently, and that she had access to a key, but I'm not sure whether she stole Emily's stuffed animals or not. When she said that she'd moved on, I believed her."

"Wow, how did you get all of that?" I asked him. "Were you listening to a different conversation than I was?"

"It was mostly a combination of body language, tone of voice, aversion of eyes, and a dozen other nonverbal signs I was watching for," he answered.

"You're a regular walking lie detector, aren't you?"

"Is that a dig at me, Suzanne?" he asked me with one raised eyebrow.

"On the contrary, it's a compliment," I replied. "I wish I had your cop's intuition."

"You do all right on your own. So, do you disagree with anything I just said?"

"No, she absolutely needs to stay on our list. I'd like to do a little more digging, but we have other folks we need to speak with first. The next one is going to be fun."

"In what way?" Jake asked.

"In a sarcastic one," I answered. "We have to speak with Hattie Moon."

"I don't know anything about her. Is that honestly her real name?"

"It would have to be, wouldn't it? Besides, it's not her name that she lies about; at least I don't think it is. Hattie has claimed to be fifty-nine years old for the past eight years that *I* know of."

"Would she really steal Emily's stuffed animals over a spat with your ex-husband?"

"She's an actress at the community theater, and if ever a woman was overdramatic, it would be her," I told him. "Remember, Emily said that Hattie claimed that she'd burn the theater down if he didn't change his mind."

"Would someone really be so mean spirited as to kidnap Emily's stuffed animals because she didn't get a role in a local production at a community theater, let alone threaten to torch the place?" Jake asked me.

"From what Max has told me, his actors and actresses take these things very seriously," I said.

"So then, we need to grill a senior citizen about three missing stuffed animals."

"That about sums it up," I said as I neared Hattie's house. "What do you think, good sir? Are you up for it?"

"With you by my side, you shouldn't even have to ask. Absolutely."

CHAPTER 5

A S WE GOT WITHIN A block of Hattie's house, my phone rang. "Hello?"

"Hi, Suzanne," a familiar voice on the other end said. "It's Jennifer."

Jennifer was the leader of our book club, and I was relieved to finally be hearing from her. Since the murder of one of our members' spouses had occurred, we hadn't had another meeting, and I was beginning to wonder if we ever would. "It's great of you to call. Have you picked a new book yet? I'm dying to get started back up."

"That's why I'm calling," she said, her voice clearly uncomfortable about responding to my question. "It looks like we're going to be skipping another month, maybe more."

I was afraid of that. "How's Elizabeth doing? I've tried calling her half a dozen times since that weekend, but I can't seem to ever reach her."

"She's difficult to connect with sometimes," Jennifer said. I had to wonder if that was true for everyone, or just for me.

"Is she coping with what happened?"

"She's doing her best. What can I say? It's been tough on her. She and Hazel are together right now, as a matter of fact."

"I wish there was something that *I* could do," I said.

"Right now she just needs some time," Jennifer said. I was about to add something when she quickly finished, "I've got to go. I'm really sorry."

"You'll be in touch though, right?" I asked.

I was talking to myself, though. The line was dead.

I frowned as I put my phone away.

When I didn't comment on the conversation, Jake decided to ask anyway. "That didn't sound like particularly good news. I'm guessing it was about your book club."

"To be honest with you, I'm not entirely sure we still have one. I don't understand. Jennifer and Hazel were there that weekend, too. Why will Elizabeth see them and not me?"

"You were quite a bit more active in her husband's murder investigation than they were," Jake said. That was an understatement. Jake and I had single-handedly solved his murder together. Shouldn't that make her embrace us instead of avoid me?

"So? What's your point?"

"Suzanne, you need to remember that the three of them were friends long before you joined the group. That weekend *we* were the outsiders, and we asked some very probing questions during our investigation. I wish I could say that it was unusual to be scorned by someone you've suspected of being a murderer, but you know the answer to that just as well as I do. I'm sorry it's happening to you, though," he added as he patted my knee.

"It is what it is, I suppose," I said. "Let's not talk about it anymore, okay? It's just making things worse."

"I can not talk about just about anything you choose," Jake said, proving his point by saying nothing else after that.

Doing my best to put my hurt feelings aside, I took a deep breath, and then I asked him, "How do you want to approach Hattie?"

"I still can't believe that's really her name. Hattie Moon? It sounds as though it's a stage name to me."

I nodded. "It's her name all right. I went to camp with a girl named April Showers. Why would parents do that to a poor kid? As for Hattie, she's quite the character."

"How well do you know her?" Jake asked me as we pulled up in front of a neat little cottage near town. Where the Jefferson place had been run-down and clearly on its last legs, Hattie's home was bright, fresh, and welcoming.

"Not that well," I admitted as I shut off the engine. "I should warn you to be prepared. She's a little melodramatic at times."

"What times in particular?" Jake asked me in all seriousness.

"Only when she's awake, I suspect," I said.

At least I knew she was home. Her tricycle, in all its glory, was parked in her carport. In lieu of a car, Hattie had opted for an adult tricycle, decked out with a basket in front, streamers on the handlebars, and even a bell to warn unsuspecting pedestrians of her presence. Well, I'm not at all certain you could call it a bell. When she pressed a button on her handlebar, a loud mooing sound emanated. I thought it was a bit odd myself, but she thought it was hilarious, mooing at folks whenever the yen grabbed her.

I knocked on the door and was surprised to see Hattie answer. Let me rephrase that. I wasn't caught off guard that she answered her own door. What shocked me was what she was wearing. Honestly, when I get into my late sixties, I hope I put away my miniskirts and tube tops, and what's more, I'm guessing all of April Springs will want the same thing. Hattie had way too much makeup on, and her hair had been teased within an inch of its life. Completing her ghastly outfit, she had on stiletto heels and thigh-high stockings, making her the perfect tart, if she were only fifty years younger.

"Hello, Hattie," I said, trying not to stare, to laugh, or to pass out from the sheer sight of her. I glanced over at Jake, who was too bug-eyed to even comment. "That's an interesting outfit you're wearing."

She actually curtsied at what she perceived to be a compliment, showing us way more of her than we needed to see. "I'm going to play Bette in our upcoming production of *Too Hot*." I'd heard about the play when it had been a hit off Broadway, but I was surprised that Max had chosen it. It wasn't because of the ages of his actors, though. Max always liked to produce seniors featured in young roles, evidenced by his *Romeo and Juliet* and *West Side Story* productions in the past. The thing is, they weren't usually so racy.

Hattie must have read my mind. "He had to tone it down quite a bit, the poor boy. He didn't want folks protesting the theater."

I remembered Emily's note, which didn't jibe with Hattie's statement. "I was under the impression that Max had cast someone else in the lead. Did he change his mind?"

"No," she said, clouding up for a moment like a petulant child. "Technically I'm Vera Grosscup's understudy, but if I know Vera, she'll drop out the night before we open. She doesn't have the moxie to play the role that I do. I was born for that part."

"I don't doubt it for one second," I said, lying with every syllable. "I understand you were peeved when Max wouldn't cast you."

"I was livid," she said, waving a heavily braceleted hand in the air. It was out of the norm for her. Usually Hattie liked muumuus without anything distracting from them. In fact, I'd seen her forego a coat in winter when she'd bought a particularly colorful one she wanted to show off. "I don't know what he was thinking."

"I understand you two had words," Jake said, finally finding his voice.

"We discussed the situation calmly and rationally as adults," she said, trying to play the entire thing down.

"You used some pretty incendiary words," I reminded her.

"Please. I was using hyperbole and exaggeration. That's all that it was."

"My understanding is that you threatened to burn the theater to the ground," I said.

"Did I? That doesn't sound a bit like me." Was she actually trying to persuade us that we had been misinformed? If I had to believe her or Emily, my money was on my friend, ten out of ten times.

"I'm curious about something. Did you happen to play any part in rebuilding Emily's store after the flood?" Jake asked. It was a neat way of asking her if she had access to a key.

"Oh, I pitched in once or twice," she said, crowing a little. "It was the civic-minded thing to do, after all."

"You didn't happen to have a key of your own to the shop, did you?" I asked her.

Apparently I hadn't been as delicate as Jake had in his questioning. "Suzanne Hart, why on earth would you care about something like that?"

"I was just curious," I said lamely.

"Not that it's any of your business, but no, I didn't. You can ask anyone." Her denial was a bit too vehement for my taste. Was she lying about the key? And if so, was it to hide her theft of Cow, Spots, and Moose?

"I'll take your word for it," I said, though I had no intention of doing that at all. "When's the last time you went by the newsstand?"

"It's been several days. I've been boycotting the place in proxy after being denied the role of my dreams."

"So, you blame Emily as well as Max?" Jake asked her. "Is that what you're saying?"

Her eyes narrowed a moment as she took my husband in. When she spoke, it was with definite ice in her voice. "I believe I'm finished discussing this with you."

"Could I have a glass of water?" I asked, pretending to cough as she started to close the door on us. "I've got a tickle in my throat." I wanted to see inside that house. Maybe she'd been careless enough to leave the stuffed animals out where I could see them.

"I'm sorry, but the place is a mess," she said, blocking my view of anything else inside. "Now if you'll excuse me, I must work on my lines."

"As an understudy," I reminded her.

"I still must be prepared to go on at a moment's notice," she said, and then she slammed the door in our faces.

"What do you think?" I asked Jake as we started back toward the Jeep.

"I think if I were Vera Grosscup, I'd have someone else taste my food before I ate it," he said with a frown.

"I'm serious."

"So am I," Jake said. "Hattie's a real prize, isn't she?"

"I don't think there's any doubt about that, but is she capable of stealing Cow, Spots, and Moose? That's the question."

"I just said in no uncertain terms that I thought she was capable of poisoning another actress to get a community theater role. Stealing three stuffed animals would be a cakewalk for her."

"So, we keep looking, but she stays on the list."

"As far as I'm concerned," Jake said with a wry grin, "she just made her way to the top."

"Save that position until we speak with Dusty," I said.

"Is he as interesting as Hattie?" Jake asked me.

"No, but if any man in town is in love with himself more than Max, it's got to be Dusty Baxter."

"This should be a real treat, then," Jake answered.

"We'll find a way to manage," I said as I drove to Dusty's place.

At least I knew where to find him. We needed to speak with him as soon as possible.

At least that was my intention at the time.

"Dusty, are you in there?" I called out after ringing his doorbell and knocking loudly as well.

"Suzanne, he's not here," Jake said as he tapped my shoulder.

"There's his Miata," I said as I pointed to his only means of transportation. "Dusty isn't exactly the walking type. If his car is in the driveway, then he's got to be around here somewhere." I tried the front door, but unlike the Jefferson house, this one was locked tight.

"Where are you going?" Jake asked me as I started walking around the house, realizing immediately that there was no way I'd ever be able to peek into the windows. The house had been built in the seventies if I had to guess, because nearly all of the windows were a good seven feet above the ground, housed in squatty wide openings. I could never live in a house like that. I needed light, but more importantly than that, I had to have a view.

"He's inside. I can feel it in my bones," I insisted. "Can you peek in and see?"

"I'm not sure that's such a great idea," he said.

"Why, because you don't want to get caught being a peeping tom?" I asked him in a gentle, teasing voice.

"No, because even if I managed to do it, which looks impossible at first glance, there are curtains everywhere."

"Why would you need curtains if your windows were so high?" I asked him.

"Maybe he's not as big a fan of light as you are," Jake offered.

"I suppose it's possible," I said. I hated being thwarted.

"Is there any chance he's at work and maybe got a ride with someone else?" Jake asked.

"Dusty doesn't have a real job," I said. "He's living off his inheritance."

"Is he rich?" Jake asked with skepticism. "If he is, he certainly chose an odd place to live."

"I didn't say it was a vast inheritance," I said. "This house belonged to his folks, and I've heard him say he owns it free and clear."

"He still needs money for other things like food, gas, utilities, and property taxes, if nothing else," Jake said.

"So maybe he got more than just the house," I said.

"Would he really steal Emily's stuffed animals?" Jake asked me as we walked back out to the Jeep.

"I can't think of a single reason that he wouldn't. Think about it. It would be a double victory for him," I said. "He'd get back at Emily for rejecting him *and* he'd make Max's life miserable at the same time. He's my favorite suspect at the moment."

"More than Michelle and Hattie?" Jake asked. "What are you basing that on?"

I shrugged. "I can't say. I've just got an inkling," I said, fully expecting him to tease me.

Instead, my husband simply nodded.

"Really? You're not going to make any comment on that statement at all?" I asked him.

"I wouldn't dream of it, Suzanne. Over the years, I've grown to respect your inklings," Jake said. "Let's see if we can figure out what Dusty is up to."

"I'm not sure how we're going to do that," I admitted.

I grabbed my car keys, but Jake put a hand on mine, stopping me. "What's wrong?"

"I might have given up too quickly," he admitted.

"Why do you say that?"

"Because you didn't tell me about your inkling before," Jake said solemnly.

"You're not making fun of me, are you?" I asked as I studied his face. If he was teasing me, he was doing a remarkable job of hiding it.

"Not a chance. Come on. Let's go back."

"What if we get run off again like we did at the Jefferson place?" I asked him. "Word is going to get around town that we're peering into strange windows without cause."

"Would anyone really be all that surprised once they found out we were looking for Emily's stuffed animals?" Jake asked me as we got out and moved to the back of the house once again.

"Probably not," I admitted. "I thought the curtains covered every window. Besides, they are too tall. You're right about that."

"Not all of them," Jake said. "I thought I saw a gap in one toward the back."

"But you still aren't tall enough to look inside, and I don't have a handy ladder in my Jeep for you to use."

"I might not need it," he said, "but I could use a hand. Come on."

"Are you going to put me on your shoulders?" I asked him.

"Truthfully, I never even thought about that," he said.

"Well, I certainly can't put you up on mine," I protested.

"You don't have to," he said with a smile. "There's a window well for the crawlspace right below one of the windows."

"What do you need me for, then?" I asked him.

"I need you to steady my legs so I don't fall," he requested.

"That I can do."

Jake started to mount the precarious thin metal semicircle buried in the ground protecting the crawlspace vent, but he quickly hopped back off.

"What's wrong?"

"It's not stable enough to hold me," he said with a frown. "It looks like we're going to have to do it your way."

"Like I said, you're not getting on my shoulders."

"That's not what I meant. You're getting on mine," he said as he squatted down.

I didn't have any better ideas, so I backed onto his shoulders, planting my rump firmly behind his neck. With one swift motion, Jake stood up, and I nearly lost my balance and fell. He grabbed me at the last second, and a moment later, I found my balance again. After taking a few careful steps, we were by the window. Jake had been right. Enough of the curtain was open so I could see inside.

It was a bedroom, but it wasn't empty.

At first I thought Dusty might be asleep, though how he'd managed not to wake up with our pounding and doorbell ringing was beyond me.

Then I noticed the blood on his chest.

What was even worse, one of Emily's stuffed cows was sitting beside him, a bloodied knife resting on one of his front hooves.

For all of the world, it appeared that Spots had committed murder, killing the man who'd kidnapped him and his two best friends, who were both staring at the deadly tableau.

CHAPTER 6

"JAKE, PUT ME DOWN," I said as I pulled away from the window.

"I've got you, Suzanne. You don't have to worry. I promise I won't drop you."

"Dusty's dead, and I know it sounds crazy, but it looks as though Spots killed him."

Jake took a step back, squatted again, and I found my feet once more, though I wasn't all that stable at the moment. "Suzanne, if this is some kind of joke, it's in bad taste, even for you."

"I'm not kidding," I told him. "Dusty is lying on the bed with a bloodstain on his chest, and Spots is sitting across from him with a knife resting on his hoof."

"How can you tell it's Spots?" Jake asked me as we both raced for the front door.

"He has a ribbon around his tail," I said. "I thought everyone knew that."

"The entire world is not as acquainted with them as you are. Call 9-1-1."

"What are you going to do while I'm doing that?" I asked him.

"Dusty might still be alive," Jake said. "I'm going in, and I'm not waiting for backup." With that, he kicked the door at the jamb with so much force that it shattered the wood as it was flung backward. Either that door was ripe for the breaking, or my husband was on some kind of adrenaline rush. As soon as the doorframe was splintered, he reached for his weapon from its ankle holster and headed in. As I dialed 9-1-1, I followed close behind him.

He gave me an angry frown for a moment when he realized that I was shadowing him, but he didn't say anything, which I decided to interpret as his acceptance of my presence.

"9-1-1. What's your emergency?"

"Somebody killed Dusty Baxter at his house," I said.

"Suzanne, is that you?"

I didn't even bother answering as I hung up. All the dispatcher would have said was that I shouldn't go inside, which I was doing anyway, so there was really no need for further instruction.

Jake quickly but thoroughly searched each room on his way to where I'd seen Dusty's body.

"He's back there," I said urgently, pointing in the direction I'd seen his body.

"I need to make sure the attacker isn't still here," Jake said patiently.

That made sense. After all, it wouldn't do Dusty any good, even if by some miracle he was still alive, for us to get ambushed trying to save him. In a few short moments Jake had finished his search of the rest of the house.

Apparently we were alone.

Jake raced to the bed as I started to reach for Spots. I hated seeing him posed with the murder weapon like that. It offended my spirit on so many levels. Jake must have seen what I was doing out of the corner of his eye. "Don't touch anything, Suzanne." He knelt down and touched Dusty's neck, searching for a pulse.

After a few moments, he stood and shook his head. "There's

no pulse, but he's still warm to the touch. Unless I miss my guess, we didn't miss the killer by more than a few minutes."

That thought chilled me to my core.

We'd just managed to avoid a confrontation with a murderer! Why kill Dusty, though? It didn't make any sense. Had he stolen Cow, Spots, and Moose, or had the killer brought them along to frame him for the theft? I had a great many more questions than answers, but I knew one thing for sure.

The theft of Cow, Spots, and Moose had gone from a bad prank to homicide, and I knew that there was no way that the police would be able to dismiss the investigation now that murder was a part of the scenario.

I wasn't sure how the three stuffed animals fit into the whole thing, but it was obvious enough that every last one of them was involved from hoof to head.

CHAPTER 7

"You've got to be kidding me," Police Chief Grant said the moment he was on the scene. He came in with his gun drawn, just as Jake had.

"It's serious enough that I wouldn't joke about it," my husband said. "Dusty is dead."

"Did either one of you happen to touch anything?" the chief asked Jake and me as he studied the body.

"We've both been putting our hands on everything in sight since we got here. Why, was that wrong?" Jake asked him, the sarcasm dripping from his voice.

"I have to ask," the chief said with a shrug.

"Me?" Jake queried.

"No. Of course not. Sorry." The chief at least had the decency to blush under my husband's scrutiny.

"I didn't touch anything either, if anyone cares," I said.

Both men looked at me with the exact same expression. I figured that my input wasn't needed at the moment, so I went back to taking in the scene. "Why would someone try to make it look as though Spots was the killer?" I asked.

"How can you be sure it's Spots?" the chief asked after looking carefully at the stuffed animal with the weapon. It sounded just as ludicrous in my head when I thought about it that way.

"It's the ribbon," I said, pointing to the frazzled and once-bright green ribbon, now faded to hold barely any color at all, tied around his tail. "Emily did that when she first got the guys."

"Why would she do that?" the chief asked.

"How else would she be able to tell them apart?" I asked him incredulously.

It was clear the police chief wasn't interested in getting into that particular discussion with me. "He's still warm to the touch," he noted.

"We noticed that, too," Jake said, being gracious enough to include me as well, though I hadn't touched Dusty's lifeless body, nor did I have any desire to confirm. I'd been forced to touch enough corpses in my life, and I wasn't about to go out of my way to touch any more of them if I could help it.

"That should at least give us a pretty tight time of death," the chief said, and I had to wonder if he was mostly talking to himself.

"I still don't understand why anyone would try to frame Spots," I said, repeating myself.

The chief said, "Suzanne, it's a stuffed animal, remember? Nobody's going to believe that it killed someone."

"I know what he is," I said, "but you can't honestly believe that the knife placement isn't significant."

"That's exactly what I believe," he said. "A mentor of mine once taught me that the world is full of people who only *think* they are funny and clever, and killers are no different."

"I didn't mean it was *always* the case," Jake said.

I'd suspected that he'd been the mentor in question, since he'd taken the current chief under his guidance when he'd held the job himself.

"Well, you can think whatever you'd like to, but *I* happen to think it's significant," I said firmly. Stephen Grant was getting a little too stuffy for my taste lately. I suppose being the chief law enforcement officer for our area was a heavy responsibility, but that shouldn't mean that he wasn't open to ideas from outside the force, even ones that initially sounded a little odd.

Chief Grant bit his lip for a moment, and then he said, "I appreciate you calling this in. We'll take it from here."

"Are you *dismissing* us?" I asked him, my ire showing a bit more than I'd wanted.

Jake clearly decided it was time to head off an argument between us.

"Suzanne, let's get out of here and let the chief do his job."

"I appreciate that," Stephen Grant said, and then, after studying my frown for a moment, he added, "Suzanne, I'm not trying to be mean to you. I just need to do things my own way."

"I understand that," I said, though I really didn't, at least not completely. "May I at least have your permission to tell Emily that her stuffed animals have been found? She's sick with worry, even if they *are* only toys left over from her childhood."

"I never said that," the chief replied quickly, "but I'd appreciate it if you'd hold off on that just for now."

"She can't do that, and it's not fair to ask her to," Jake said, surprising me by speaking up in my defense.

"You're not going to start giving me trouble too now, are you?" Chief Grant asked him.

"I'm not saying a word to anyone, but you can't expect Suzanne to keep quiet about this. She genuinely cares for Emily, and I know for a fact that there's no way she's not going to tell her about this."

The chief frowned for a few moments before he finally spoke. "How about this? You can tell Emily you found her pals." I was about to thank him when he held up a finger to signify that he wasn't finished yet. "You just can't tell anyone about the knife."

"I didn't think you believed that it was even significant," I said a little starkly.

"I don't, but only one other person knows about this besides the three of us, and I mean to keep it that way." As we watched, he took some photos of Spots, the knife, and everything around them. Once he was satisfied with the shots he'd gotten, he took out an evidence bag, turned it inside out, and then he put his hand inside and collected the knife.

"Should you really have done that?" Jake asked him in a surprised voice, clearly a little startled by the man's actions.

"Maybe not, but the positioning of the knife is knowledge that is limited to only four people. By the time my crew gets in and photographs everything, the entire town is going to know what we found. Do you honestly think I should put it back before anyone gets here?" There was a shade of doubt in his voice as he asked the question, reminding me of the beat cop I'd known once upon a time before he'd taken on so much responsibility.

"No, it's a bold idea and a gamble worth taking, and it might just turn out to be worth the risk," Jake said.

It clearly wasn't the ringing endorsement the chief had been looking for, but it was going to have to do. "I promise that we won't tell anyone about that part," I said.

"Good," he replied. He was still staring at the knife in his hands ten seconds later when one of his deputies came in.

The chief was about to speak when Jake touched my arm. "Come on, Suzanne. Let's go."

"Are you sure you don't want to hang around for just a bit more?" I asked him.

"I'm sure," Jake replied. Once we were outside, he said, "Suzanne, Chief Grant could get into a great deal of trouble if anyone found out about what he did in there."

"You wouldn't have done it yourself, would you?" I asked him.

"I can't say. I'm not in that position," he said with a shrug.

It was a surprisingly vague answer. "But you once were in exactly that position."

"The point is that I'm not now," he said with a quick shake

of his head. "You might as well give up, because that's *all* that I'm going to say on the subject. Now let's get going."

"Where to?" I asked him.

"You want to tell Emily about finding the guys, don't you?" Jake asked me.

"I thought I'd just call her," I said, surprised by my husband's attitude.

"Trust me, news like this is always better in person," he said.

"Jake, what are you up to?"

"What do you mean?" he asked me much too quickly.

"Why do you want to see Emily's reaction when we tell her about Dusty and the guys?" I asked him.

He merely shrugged, but it wasn't a response I was in any mood to accept from him.

"Jake, you don't honestly think Emily had anything to do with Dusty's murder, do you?"

"Suzanne, I like her nearly as much as you do, but that doesn't give her a free pass here. Emily needs to be on our list of suspects."

"But we found the stuffed animals," I said. "Isn't the case over?"

"That one is, sort of, but we've got something a lot bigger on our hands now."

"Are we going to try to solve Dusty's murder?" I asked my husband.

"I thought we might. Are you up for it?"

"I am if you are," I said without hesitation.

"Even if the trail leads us somewhere you don't want to go?" he asked a little pointedly.

"The truth is what matters. I don't for one second think Emily killed Dusty, even if he was the one who stole her stuffed animals, but if she did, she has to pay for it, just like anyone else would."

"Then let's go have a chat with her and see how she reacts to the news that Dusty is dead and her stuffed animals have been recovered."

The only problem with our plan was that Emily wasn't at the newsstand when we got there. Christine frowned a moment when we walked in and asked about her daughter. "Was she expecting you? I hadn't realized you were meeting her here."

"We didn't think we'd have to call ahead for an appointment," I said with a smile. "Do you have any idea when she'll be back?"

"I don't know. She didn't say," Christine replied.

"Where exactly did she go?" Jake asked as nonchalantly as he could. He'd come a long way in changing his inquiries from demands for information to requests, but he wasn't quite there yet.

"Why do you need to speak with her? Did something happen?" Christine asked, the worry coming through in her voice.

"Yes," Jake and I said at the same time.

"You two need to stop playing and tell me exactly what's going on," Christine insisted.

If we did that, she would without a doubt call her daughter and ruin any chance we would have to surprise her with the information. I wasn't expecting to catch Emily looking guilty, even if Jake might be, but an honest and unplanned reaction would help her case with my husband. I couldn't see Emily killing someone no matter what the circumstances might be, and as much as she loved her stuffed animals, it certainly wasn't motivation enough to commit a homicide. "I'll call her myself," I said as I grabbed my phone.

"I don't like this," Christine said as she pulled her own phone out of her pocket.

I put a hand on hers. "Do you believe that I'm trying to help your daughter, and that all I'm trying to find is the truth?" I asked her before either one of us could place our calls.

"I suppose so," Christine said a little reluctantly.

"Then let me do this my way," I replied. I knew if I called Emily and she saw that her mother was calling her as well, I'd lose that battle every time. To be fair, I would have done the same thing to her if it had been my mother calling me instead.

It took Christine three seconds to decide, three very long seconds, but finally, she put her phone away. "Suzanne, I'm trusting you to look out for my daughter's best interests."

"I won't let you down," I replied, hoping that I wouldn't be forced to do just that.

"I'm going to hold you to that."

I dialed Emily's number, but she didn't answer.

"Huh. She didn't pick up."

"Now *I'm* getting worried," Christine said. "Let me try."

Even as she made the offer to call her daughter for me, my cell phone rang. When I glanced at the caller ID, I said with relief, "It's Emily," and then I answered it.

"Hey, Emily."

"Sorry about that, Suzanne. I wanted to pull over. I know it's legal to talk on your cell phone in your car in North Carolina, but I get too distracted when I try to talk and drive at the same time. What's up? Have you had any luck finding the guys?"

"How far from the newsstand are you right now?" I asked her, sidestepping her question.

"Less than two minutes," she said. "Why?"

"We need to talk about this in person." I didn't want to give her any more information than I had to.

"That doesn't sound good," she said. "You really have to tell me what's going on right now."

"I'll see you in two minutes," I said, and then I hung up on her. It was the hardest thing I'd done in a long time, but if I told her what was going on over the phone, we couldn't see her reaction to the news. I wanted to protect my friend, just as I'd promised Christine, but I also didn't want to waylay our investigation of Dusty's murder. It was a fine line I was walking, and I wasn't a bit sure I could do it for very long.

"She'll be here in a minute," I told Christine and Jake.

"So we heard," Christine said. "Why didn't you tell her while you had her on the phone?"

"Did you really want me to tell her something as huge as that on the phone?" I asked her.

"No, I suppose not. I'm still not sure why you won't tell me, though."

She had a point, but I wasn't going to concede it. I couldn't, at least not without telling her what I was holding back from her.

Thankfully, Emily walked into Two Cows and a Moose ninety seconds later. At least there were no customers in the shop. That could have been a little awkward asking them to leave so we could have a private conversation.

"What is it?" Emily said as she pulled off her jacket. "Did you find them?"

"As a matter of fact, we did," I said.

Her face lit up like a kid's might on Christmas morning. "That's absolutely glorious. I'm so happy I could cry." She looked up at their shelf, but it was still empty. As her gaze scanned the room, she asked me in a puzzled voice, "Why aren't they here?"

"They are in police custody at the moment," I said.

"What did they do, knock over a gas station?" Emily asked. "Seriously, where are they? I need to see them for myself."

"Emily, we found them at the scene of a murder," I said, watching her carefully.

She looked at me for a moment as though I had just told a bad joke. "Suzanne, that's not at all funny."

"It wasn't meant to be. Emily, Dusty Baxter is dead."

CHAPTER 8

"**D**EAD? WHAT DO YOU MEAN he's dead?" Emily stumbled back a little at the news. I'd been watching her carefully, and her reaction wasn't quite what I'd been expecting. For a split second, it looked as though she hadn't been completely shocked by the news.

That was bad.

I glanced over at Jake and saw that her reaction hadn't gone unnoticed.

"We found him at his home. Someone stabbed him in the chest with a knife," Jake explained.

Emily took a moment to recover. "That's terrible, but what does it have to do with Cow, Spots, and Moose? Did *Dusty* steal them?"

"We don't know yet," I said. "It might be a good working assumption for the moment until we learn differently, though."

"Why are the police keeping the guys, though? I don't understand." Emily finally looked as though she was going to cry, something that her mother noticed before I did. Christine quickly moved to her daughter and put her arm around her shoulder, offering her what comfort she could.

I couldn't exactly tell Emily that Spots had been holding the murder weapon. Jake and I had promised the police chief to keep that particular tidbit to ourselves. "They were at the scene of the crime. I'm sure you'll get them soon."

"I hope they are okay," Emily said. I knew she loved her

stuffed animals, but was that really her main concern about the situation? Was she in shock, or was the statement more telling than she'd intended it to be?

"From what we saw, they weren't any worse for the wear from the experience," I admitted. Jake frowned at me and shook his head slightly. It was clear that he was afraid I might let something slip out about how we'd found them, but I had made a promise to the police chief, and I wasn't about to break it. "Emily, when we spoke earlier, you said something about Dusty that puzzled me."

"What did I say?" she asked haltingly. "I just can't get over the fact that he's dead."

"You told me to be careful around Dusty, that he wasn't as harmless as he looked. What exactly did you mean by that?"

"I don't remember saying that at all," Emily said evasively, refusing to make eye contact with me as she answered.

She was clearly lying to me! At least she wasn't very good at it, which meant to me that she probably hadn't had that much practice doing it. "Think, Emily. It's important."

"I don't believe I like the tone of voice you are taking with my daughter, young lady," Christine said as she stepped between us. I knew that she was just trying to protect her only child. I couldn't blame her, but on the other hand, she was making matters worse instead of better. I firmly believed that if I gave Emily time to adjust to what had happened, she would probably have time to think of a reason to explain her earlier comment to me. Was it possible that she was involved in Dusty's murder after all? I didn't want to think it was even within the realm of possibility, but even *I* was beginning to have my doubts.

"Christine, whether you like it or not, Emily is involved in this investigation up to her eyebrows. We need to find out what's happening if we're going to help her." It was an appeal that I hoped would work. Otherwise, I knew we weren't going to be getting much out of Emily from here on out.

"Why is *she* a part of it?" Christine asked icily. "She barely knew the man. So what if they dated for a time? It was ill conceived and promptly ended." Apparently no man was good enough for her daughter, but I could see Christine's objections to both Dusty and Max.

"Mom, would you do me a favor?" Emily asked.

"Anything," Christine said. "Would you like me to ask them to leave? You don't need this kind of questioning."

"As a matter of fact, I was hoping you'd run home and make me a cup of your famous hot chocolate, and grab an oatmeal raisin cookie or two while you're there. I desperately need some comfort food right now."

"*Now*? Surely a snack can wait until later," Christine said. She was clearly unhappy about abandoning her daughter in her time of need.

"It's the *only* thing in the world that might make me feel better right now," Emily said. "Please? For me?"

"Of course. I'd do anything for you," Christine said. As she started for the door, she gave it one last shot to try to get us to leave as well. "Surely you two have somewhere else you need to be. We wouldn't want to keep you."

"Mother. Please." Emily uttered the two words, and Christine knew that she'd lost that last battle as well.

"I'll be right back then," she said, trying to make her voice light and carefree, but not before stopping directly in front of me and adding, "Remember your promise to me, Suzanne."

"I remember," I said.

Once she was gone, Emily asked me point blank, "What did she make you promise?"

"She made me swear that I'd look after your best interests," I admitted. "Which, in my defense, I'm trying to do."

Emily frowned upon hearing the news. "Why would she ask you to do something like that? Suzanne, she knows that we've been friends for years. My question is why *wouldn't* you look out for me?"

"I'm going to do my best, but for me to do that, for us to do that," I corrected as I gestured toward Jake, "we need to know the truth."

"I wouldn't lie to you," she said, avoiding my gaze yet again.

"Emily, stop it." My voice was probably a little harder than it had to be, but I needed to get her attention.

"Stop what?" she asked, still unable to meet my stare.

"Stop lying to us, and I mean this instant," I said.

"What makes you think I'm lying?" Emily asked me, still avoiding all eye contact. I was no expert at reading people, but she might as well have been holding up a sign that said, "Liar!"

"Because you're really bad at it," I said as nicely as I could. "Trust me, that's a good thing. We need to know the truth if we're going to help you." I looked over at Jake. "Am I right?"

"You are," Jake said, keeping his comment to a minimum. My husband knew that Emily was my friend, so I should be the one handling the interview, unless and until he thought I was about to bungle it. So far, so good, then. I couldn't let my relationship with Emily affect how I conducted this investigation. If I hurt her feelings now, there would be time later to mend fences and make amends, but right now, I needed the truth, for the very reason that I'd just told her.

Without it, I couldn't help her.

"Where have you been for the last half hour?" I asked her, trying to take things in a different direction for a moment. "Remember, we need to know the truth, no matter how badly it might reflect on you." Maybe if I asked her a few easier questions, it would loosen her up and make her more willing to talk to us about Dusty and what had happened to him. Besides, I wanted to know if she had an alibi for Dusty's time of death. "We asked, and your mother had no idea where you went."

"I was just driving around in the country, hoping to figure out who would want to hurt me badly enough to steal my stuffed animals," she said after a few moments of silence.

"Did anyone happen to see you while you were out?" Jake asked her gently.

"How could I possibly know that?" she asked him critically.

"What Jake is trying to determine is if you stopped and spoke with anyone while you were gone. Did you even wave to someone you made eye contact with somewhere along the way?"

It took Emily a moment, but she got it. "Are you asking me for an alibi?" she asked me, the hurt clear in her voice.

"We're trying to help you," I said. "You can't look at this as though we're coming after you, Emily. If someone saw you on your drive, we can tell the police and clear you of all suspicion."

"Does the *chief* think I'm involved?" she asked, surprised by the very idea.

"Your stuffed animals, the three things that are closest to your heart, were stolen from you," Jake reminded her. "They were found at the murder scene. He wouldn't be doing his job if he didn't at least consider you a possible suspect."

"If I'd killed Dusty, I certainly wouldn't have left my stuffed animals there," Emily said, the tears creeping into her voice. "I couldn't have done that to them."

"You might have if you were rushed, or stunned by the suddenness of what happened," Jake suggested lightly.

"Is that what you think?" Emily asked him.

"As your friend? No, of course not. As a former cop, though? I'd be lying if I said it wouldn't have crossed my mind."

Emily buried her head in her hands, and I felt really bad for her. I hated pushing her about such painful things, but I knew that sooner rather than later, Chief Grant would have to speak with her about her three friends and where they'd been found, and he would be a lot tougher on her than we were being.

"I can't prove where I was," Emily finally said, her voice heavy with sadness. "I'm sorry I don't have some convenient alibi, but it's the truth, so do with it what you may."

"Let's get back to my other question," I said before she could start crying again. "What did you mean when you told me that Dusty wasn't as harmless as he looked? Don't bother trying to deny it again. We both know that you said it, so don't insult our friendship by trying to claim now that you didn't."

"I shouldn't have said anything to you about it. It was a mistake," she said almost to herself.

"Maybe so, but you can't just dismiss it like that. Did something happen between the two of you?" I asked her without letting up on her. It felt a little heartless pushing her so hard, but if she told us the truth, we might just be able to help her, at least if she were truly innocent, which I wanted to believe was true with all of my heart.

I didn't think Emily was going to answer, but finally, after taking enough time to collect herself, she admitted, "He was here at the newsstand last night."

"What happened?" I asked softly. Jake was listening intently, but it was obvious that he was going to continue to let me handle the questioning. I was fine with that. After all, I'd been friends with Emily for a long time, and with that friendship, there had grown an element of trust that I hoped I wasn't currently violating.

"Dusty came by last night as I was closing the shop," she

said. "No one else was around, and he told me that he still had feelings for me. When I rejected him and told him that I was in love with Max, he said that I was being a child, that I didn't know what I wanted. Dusty told me that it didn't have to be about love between us, that it could be something physical without any emotion. I laughed at the suggestion, which I immediately realized was a mistake. He pinned me against the wall, and when he put his face within half an inch of mine, he told me that it wasn't nice to laugh at him, and I was going to have to pay for that. I thought he was going to do something horrible, and if someone hadn't opened the door of the shop and that chime hadn't gone off, I'm still not sure what he would have done."

"Someone witnessed the attack?" Jake asked. I knew the situation could incriminate Emily in Dusty's death, and so did Jake. "Did you see who it was?"

"They never came all the way in, and the way Dusty had me pinned against the wall, I couldn't see who it was."

"Did *Dusty* know who it was?" I asked.

"He clearly recognized whoever it was," Emily explained. "The second they left, he let me go and tried to brush it off as though nothing had happened. When he started to leave, I felt a surge of relief that I was going to escape with my life, but then he hesitated at the door, turned to me, and said, 'If you tell anyone about this, I'll kill you, and your parents, and everyone and everything you love.' It shook me up more than the assault had. He was so calm and nonchalant when he said it! I was terrified to say a word to anyone, so I didn't."

"Not even to Max?" I asked.

"Especially not to him," she said. "You know what kind of temper he has. He would have killed Dusty with his bare hands if he'd seen him assaulting me."

"I wouldn't tell anyone else that," Jake said. "They might take it the wrong way."

"It's okay. Max isn't here, remember?" she asked. "He's in Los Angeles."

"Are you saying that you didn't even *call* him? If I'd been in your shoes, I would have phoned Jake instantly," I said.

"I tried," Emily said, her voice faltering. "I wasn't going to tell him about Dusty and his threat, but I needed to hear his voice. He didn't pick up, though."

"Did you call his hotel or his cell phone?" Jake asked her.

"His cell phone," she said, frowning again. "Why would I call his hotel?"

"I'm just curious. Where is he staying?"

"Max always stays at the Restchester when he's in LA," she said. "Anyway, I went home and went to bed. I'd say I went to sleep, but I got precious little of that. When I came in this morning to open the shop, the guys were gone, and I found the ransom note I gave you. I swear to you both that last night was the final time I ever saw Dusty Baxter, dead or alive. I hope you believe me."

"What we believe doesn't matter," Jake said.

It might have been the right thing to say as a cop, but it wasn't anywhere close to being what a friend should say. I took Emily's hands in mine. "Believe me, we are going to do everything in our power to find the truth about what happened to Dusty."

"Does that mean that you don't believe me, either?" she asked me, her voice trembling as she asked the question. "Suzanne, it's important to me that you don't think of me as a murderer."

"Emily, Jake didn't phrase it the way I would have, but what he said was true enough. What matters right now is what we can prove and what we can speculate, not what we feel. If we start eliminating suspects just because we love them, there wouldn't even be a reason to investigate. We have to clear our emotions away and look at the facts. You and I have been friends for a very long time, and if there's anything my husband and I can do to help you, we will, as long as you didn't kill Dusty."

"Of course I didn't kill him!"

"Take a deep breath," I said. "I didn't accuse you of anything. If you're innocent, you don't have anything to worry about from us. We'll do everything in our power to make sure that the real killer is caught."

"Okay, I guess I can see the distinction," she said after a moment. "What can I do to help you make it happen and make this cloud over my life go away?"

"Be honest with everyone you speak with. Don't try to hide anything from the police when you talk to them like you just did with us," Jake answered before I could.

"Even if it makes me look guilty?" she asked incredulously.

"Believe me, I fully understand that no one likes to put themselves in a compromising position, but the chief needs to know what happened. If that witness comes forward and tells the chief what he saw and heard before you tell him yourself, it's going to make you look ten times as guilty as if you volunteer the information up front."

"Do you really think the police are going to come here and start grilling me about Dusty's murder?" she asked, clearly worried about the prospect of a full-on interrogation.

"Honestly, I'm a little surprised they haven't been here already," Jake said just as the front door chime went off.

We all turned to the door and were each in turn equally surprised that it was just Christine, back bearing a thermos and a piece of Tupperware large enough to contain at least a dozen of the requested cookies. The treats were quickly forgotten, abandoned with the thermos on the counter, as she spotted her daughter's tears. "What's going on here?"

"It's okay, Mom," Emily said as she started to wipe the tears from her face.

"It is *anything* but okay, young lady," Christine told her daughter. She marched straight toward us as if she were about to do battle, which in a very real sense, she was. "You two need to leave."

"Mom, they're only trying to help," Emily protested, but her voice was a little weak as she said it.

"Then they can do it someplace else." Christine stood directly in front of me, and though she bore little resemblance to my own mother, her stance and the determined expression on her face were both all too familiar. "I mean it. Good-bye."

I nodded in capitulation without even looking at Jake. I knew that we'd gotten all that we could out of Emily at the moment, and with Christine acting as her guardian, it wouldn't do us any good to try to keep questioning her. "We're going, but Christine, we're just trying to help Emily."

"Then help her by leaving," she said.

Jake and I started to walk out when I turned to Emily and added, "If you need me, I'm just a phone call away."

"She won't need you. She's got me," Christine said firmly.

We were out on the sidewalk before Jake said a word. "Was it just me, or did she remind you of your mother just then?"

I laughed a little despite the seriousness of the situation. "It wasn't just you. She had a definite 'defending lioness' vibe going on there. Not that I can blame her. It must have looked as though we were attacking her daughter when she walked in, even though we were just trying to help her."

"To an extent, at any rate," Jake said as we got in the Jeep.

"What do you mean by that?" I asked, hesitating before I started the engine.

"Suzanne, if Emily killed Dusty and we can prove it, we aren't going to be helping her at all," Jake said.

"Do you really think she did it?" I asked him.

"I don't know yet," he said. "I just want to make it clear that if we find proof that she did it, we're turning our evidence over to the police. Agreed?"

"I wouldn't dream of doing anything else," I said. "I'm kind of surprised you'd even ask me that, Jake."

"Suzanne, I know how loyal you are to your friends."

"I'd walk through fire for them," I agreed, "but if I discovered that one of them had committed murder, I'd do everything in my power to make sure they paid for the crime. Otherwise I'd never be able to look at myself in the mirror again."

"That's what I thought, but I didn't think it would hurt to be sure," he said.

"Now that we've cleared that up, what's our next step?" I asked him as I started the Jeep.

"I want to speak with Hattie and Michelle again," Jake said, "and I'd like to get to them before they find out what happened to Dusty."

"Any preferences on which one we tackle first?" I asked, happy that we had something constructive to do.

"You pick," he said. "I just need to make a quick phone call first."

"You're not calling the chief, are you?" I asked him.

Jake stopped before he could finish the call. "And if I am?"

"Fine. Just don't tell him what Emily told us."

Jake scowled for a moment before he spoke. "Suzanne, it could be a piece of critical evidence. He needs to know."

"I'm in full agreement on the point, but doesn't Emily have the right to tell him herself first?"

"If she'll actually do it," Jake said. "Don't forget, she tried to hide it from us. What makes you think she'll be more forthcoming with the police?"

"Because we told her she needed to be honest with them," I said.

"Do you really have that much faith in your friend to do the right thing?" Jake asked me as I drove back to Michelle's office. I'd decided to tackle her first mostly because she was the closest to us at the moment. Neither woman would be a treat to tackle again so soon, but we really didn't have any choice. Time really wasn't our friend at that point.

"I do. Besides, if she doesn't tell him, then we will," I said, "but let's at least give her the chance."

Jake put his phone away, albeit a bit reluctantly. "Okay. We'll play it your way for now."

"Thanks. Now let's go talk to Michelle about Dusty Baxter. It might just prove to be an interesting conversation."

CHAPTER 9

"**S**ERIOUSLY?" SHE ASKED US AS we came back into the accounting office where Michelle worked. "Is there even really a raffle? Because if there is, I'm not interested in buying any tickets from either one of you." She turned back toward her employers' offices. "They're all out at a big meeting, so you won't be able to peddle any to them, either."

"We're not here about the raffle. We need to talk about Dusty Baxter," I said.

Michelle definitely reacted to the name. "What about him? Has he been spreading more lies around town about me? Fine. I admit it. He broke my heart a few days ago. Isn't that enough for him? Why does he have to keep rubbing my nose in it? What is wrong with men? First Max and then Dusty. What kind of hold does Emily Hargraves have over them? She's not all that much to look at, is she? It's absolutely baffling. Well, she can have them both as far as I'm concerned. I'm swearing off men for the immediate future. Let's see how they like that. Max and Dusty both could walk through that door in ten seconds, and I'd send them both packing."

"Dusty didn't say anything directly to me about the two of you, and for the record, neither did Max, for what it's worth," I said, which was the absolute truth, though by no means all of it.

"I don't know why not. Dusty has been telling everyone else that I threw a fit when he dumped me, like it's some kind of badge of honor to be with him. Have you ever been in love and have someone tromp all over your heart?" Michelle paused for a moment, and then a look of sympathy briefly crossed her face. "Look who I'm asking. Of course you have. Suzanne, after what Max did to you, I never thought you'd pile on me with the rest of them."

"I'm not here to taunt you," I said. "Michelle, Dusty's dead."

Her reaction was immediate, and it somehow felt quite genuine to me. The look of puzzlement on her face quickly shattered into one of despair. "No. He can't be. I don't believe you!" She shrieked the words out loudly enough to get everyone's attention within half a mile, and I was suddenly glad that her bosses were out of the office at the moment. It took a moment or two to settle down, and when she did, she asked plaintively, "What happened? Was it a car wreck? I always told him that he drove too fast, but he would never listen to me."

"Actually, someone stabbed him in the heart," I said. I assumed the only thing the police chief was holding back was that the knife had been found in Spots's possession. I glanced at Jake with a questioning look, and he nodded his approval toward me for divulging the cause of death. It was nice to have such a high level of unspoken communication with my husband.

She nearly fell when she heard the news, just as Emily had, and if Jake hadn't been there to catch her, I'm not so sure that she wouldn't have landed hard on the floor. "I don't understand. Who would want to kill him?"

"That's exactly what we're trying to find out," I said.

"You should talk to Emily Hargraves," Michelle said angrily.

"What makes you suggest that? I thought she was still with Max," I said, trying to act as innocent as I could. Emily had told us about her confrontation with Dusty, but the real question was, had Dusty told Michelle?

"Why do you think Dusty broke up with me? He told me that he was going to win Emily back no matter what it took. I tried to tell him that he was as delusional as the rest of them, but he wouldn't listen to me!"

"When was the last time *you* saw Dusty, Michelle?" Jake asked her gently.

"Do you think *I* did it?" the receptionist shrieked, jumping to the conclusion instantly. "I loved that man, even if he *did* crush my heart. I wouldn't have hurt him for anything. Now get out of here!"

I was about to try to calm her down when the front door opened and two men and a woman walked in. They'd been smiling and joking about something, but Michelle's reaction to my question killed any levity they may have been feeling at the time.

"What's going on here?" Harvey Bascomb looked anything but friendly as he asked the question.

"Dusty is dead," she told him, breaking into sobs and throwing herself at him. As she drove her face into his chest, it was pretty clear that this particular interview was over.

"I'm so sorry, my dear," he said as he stroked her hair, doing his best to comfort her.

"If we could just ask a few more questions, we might be able to sort this out as far as Michelle is concerned," Jake said.

I glanced over at him and shook my head, but it was too late. Evidently our unspoken communication didn't go as far as ESP.

"I'm sorry, but I need to ask you both to leave," Harvey said angrily. "Don't you see that you've upset this child enough already?"

"With all due respect, sir, the police are going to be a lot tougher on her than we are," Jake said. I hadn't been surprised by his reaction. My husband believed that when you were pushed, you pushed back. It worked for him most of the time, but this wasn't going to be the case today, and I knew it before Harvey said another word.

"Then we'll deal with them when and if they come," he said. "Are you going to leave now, or must I call them myself and have you forcibly removed?"

I could see Jake tense up, but I beat him to the punch. "We were just leaving," I said. Before we departed, I looked at Michelle, who still had her head buried in the chest of one of her bosses. "We truly are sorry for your loss. The *only* thing we want to do is uncover who killed Dusty. If you loved him as much as you say you did, you'd want the same thing."

Her only response was a heightened moan, so we left before the three accountants tried to throw us out themselves.

"We should have pushed her a little harder," Jake said. "She was close to cracking."

"Jake, I love you dearly; you know that, don't you?"

"Yes. Of course. What's that got to do with anything?"

"Sometimes it seems as though you've forgotten that you're not a cop anymore. No one has to tell us anything. They were quite within their rights asking us to leave just then."

"It sounded more like a demand than a request to me," Jake said with a frown. "I don't like being told what I can and cannot do." I had to laugh at that statement, something he didn't react well to at all. "Suzanne, do you think that's *funny*?"

"Jake, *nobody* likes that happening to them. Unfortunately, we just have to deal with it and move on." I had to get him to forget about what had just happened with the accountants and deal with the task at hand. "What do you think of Michelle's reaction?"

"It felt a little too melodramatic to me, as though she'd staged it," Jake said.

"Seriously?" I asked him. "That's odd. It felt genuine to me."

"Huh. I wonder if it might be because she struck a sore nerve with you," he said softly.

It took me a few seconds to figure out what he was talking about. "Do you mean what she said about Max? Jake, it was painful, there's no doubt about it, but if he hadn't done it, I would have never found you. How many times do I have to tell you that before you believe me?"

Jake surprised me by taking me in his arms and kissing me soundly. "That should just about do it," he said after he broke our kiss.

I laughed again, but this time out of sheer happiness. When I turned toward the Jeep, I glanced back at the office and found one of the accountants watching us through a slit in the blinds. I winked at him, and the opening quickly closed. "Come on, sport, let's go see if Hattie has anything interesting to add to our pool of knowledge."

"I can't even guess as to how she's going to react. Of our two main suspects, she's the more melodramatic of the two," he said with the shake of his head.

"One can only imagine," I said.

As I drove toward Hattie's place, I glanced over at Jake and saw that he was frowning. "What's wrong? Are you thinking about the case?"

"Yes."

Seriously? Was that suddenly his idea of what a conversation was supposed to be? What happened to give and take, sharing our thoughts? "You're going to have to give me something more than that, mister," I said.

"I could tell you, but you aren't going to like it." He was looking out the side window now, avoiding any eye contact with me at all.

"You think Emily killed Dusty," I said flatly. I hated the thought of entertaining even the remotest possibility that it was true, but I knew that my husband was better able to look at a case dispassionately and evaluate the information we had than I was. Most of the time I admired the trait, but not when it concerned one of my dearest friends.

"No. At least not at the moment. That's all subject to change, though."

"You don't have to use a disclaimer with me," I said. "No one's printing this conversation in the newspaper." I glanced in the backseat as a joke. "At least I don't see Ray Blake anywhere close by, but who knows? He could be really good at hiding." Ray was not only my assistant Emma's father, but he also ran the town newspaper.

"I doubt it," was all that he said.

Again with the short answers that really didn't answer anything.

That was about all that I was willing to take. I pulled the Jeep over and turned off the engine. I'd waited for a parking lot, and the first one I'd found was at the Baptist church.

"Why are we stopping here?" Jake asked me as I pulled the key out of the ignition.

"We're not going anywhere until you talk to me."

"Suzanne, I could tell you what's on my mind, but I don't want to get into an argument with you about it."

I was more curious than anything else at that point. "What if I promise not to react one way or another to whatever you tell me?"

Jake laughed, but there wasn't any joy in it. "How could you possibly promise me that?"

"Try me." I meant it, too. He could say anything short of directly accusing my mother of the murder, and I wasn't going to even raise an eyebrow, let alone my voice.

"Okay, but remember, you're the one who pushed it. I know you and Max are on good terms, but are we absolutely sure that he's still in LA filming a commercial?"

I started to protest as an instant reaction, but my recent promise made me take a breath and then a beat. After a few moments, I asked him, "What makes you wonder that?"

"That mysterious stranger who interrupted Dusty pinning Emily at the newsstand. What if it was Max?"

"I would think if he'd been there, my ex would have raced in and tried to beat Dusty within an inch of his life," I said.

"What if he misinterpreted what he saw, though?" Jake asked.

"What do you mean?" My husband had clearly given this some thought, and I believed it was only fair to hear him out, despite my core belief that Max couldn't have ignored the situation if his life depended on it.

"What if he thought Emily was a willing participant to the embrace? Would he still rush in to confront them? I'm asking you because you know him better than anyone else."

"Maybe anyone but Emily," I amended. I thought about the scenario Jake had laid out, and I had to admit that it was a possibility. Max would have been hurt if he thought Emily was cheating on him, and he could have run away in reaction to it. That possible scenario actually played out in my head for a moment before I spoke again. "I suppose it's possible," I said, "but it's a moot point, since Max isn't even in town."

"Maybe he isn't, but then again, maybe he came back early," Jake said as he pulled out his cell phone.

"Who are you calling? You don't have Max's number in your phone, do you?" For some reason, the idea that my current husband had my ex on speed dial unsettled me.

"Relax. I'm dialing Information," he said as he held up one finger to silence me.

Normally I wouldn't have complied with that request, but I was too curious to see where he was headed to interrupt.

"The Restchester," he said, and I nodded. Emily had told us that was where Max always stayed when he was in LA. "Connect me, please."

After a moment, he asked for Max's room.

"Since when? Okay. Thanks."

After Jake disconnected the call, he said in an even voice, "Max checked out two days ago."

"Maybe he moved to another hotel," I suggested.

"Or maybe he got fired and came back early," Jake speculated. "Is that anywhere in the realm of possibility?"

"Oh, yes. Max has been fired from more jobs than he's finished," I admitted after remembering how frustrated I used to get with him for constantly sabotaging his own career.

"I wonder if I can pull some strings to see if he flew back home early," Jake mused aloud. "I have some friends who moved to Homeland Security who might be able to help."

"Hold on there, partner," I said. "I've got an easier way to find out than that."

"You have connections like that?" Jake asked with surprise.

"No, I know someone even better," I said. I called Nina Garringer, a customer of mine who was a huge fan of pumpkin donuts. Every fall she'd order a dozen a week until they were nearly gone, and then, in one last rush of glory, she'd commission me to make ten dozen just for her. Those promptly went into her freezer, and she hoarded them until pumpkin donut season came around again. Nina also happened to be Max's current landlord. Max, along with a few other folks, rented rooms from Nina, a relatively new occupation the widow had been forced into after her husband's sudden death.

"Nina, it's Suzanne Hart."

"You don't have to identify yourself to me, sweetie. What's up?"

"I was wondering if you could tell me if Max is back in town," I said.

"No."

What was it with short answers to the questions I was asking today? "No as in you can't tell me, or no as in he's still in L.A.?" I asked her.

"You knew about that?"

"We keep in touch," I said. "Please?"

Nina's voice lowered as she replied, "It's on the hush-hush. I'm not supposed to tell anyone."

"What if I guess?" I suggested.

"There's no law against that," she said, laughing a little at my suggestion.

"Did Max get fired from the commercial and come back early, but he didn't want to have to explain it to Emily or anyone else, so he asked you to keep quiet about it?"

There was nothing but dead silence.

"Nina?" I asked. "Are you still there?"

"I am."

"Well, how's my theory?"

"We never came up with a code," Nina explained.

I laughed for a moment. "You are absolutely right. Okay, how's this? If I'm right, comment on the weather. If I'm wrong, tell me I've got the wrong number. Those choices are innocent enough, aren't they?"

"I don't think it's going to rain today, but those clouds are pretty dark, so it might. You just can't tell these days, can you?"

"Thanks, Nina. Is he there right now?"

"I'm sorry, but you've got the wrong number," she said, and then she whispered, "Bye, Suzanne. Mum's the word, remember?"

"I'll remember," I said.

Jessica Beck

"You were right," I told Jake after I hung up. "Max got fired and came home early. He could have killed Dusty, couldn't he?"

"Let's not jump to conclusions," Jake said. "Just because he was in town doesn't mean anything just yet."

"It means he needs to be on our list of suspects," I corrected him.

"True. But first we have to find him. Did Nina know where he was at the moment, by any chance?"

"No, but I have a few ideas of my own about that. I need to make a few phone calls, and that's going to take some time. Should we go ahead and look for him, or should we wait until after we talk to Hattie?" I asked as I started the Jeep back up.

"Ordinarily I'd say we should delay Hattie and find Max first, but something in my gut tells me that we should go ahead and speak with her before we do anything else. After that, we can look for Max all we want." Jake paused, and then he added, "Maybe we can grab a bite at the Boxcar in between while you're making your calls."

"Sounds good to me," I said. "I'm starving, too."

As I drove to Hattie's place, I couldn't help wondering if Max had indeed committed murder. It wasn't something I wanted to even consider, but what choice did I have? If he felt as though he'd lost everything he'd ever really cared about, he just might have done it. I needed to speak with him and hear him declare his innocence directly, but before I could do that, Jake and I needed to talk to Hattie.

There would be time to talk to Max soon enough if I was ever able to track him down. When my ex didn't want to be found, he was very, very good at hiding, but he'd met his match with me.

At least I hoped so.

78

CHAPTER 10

"**H**ER TRICYCLE IS GONE," I said as I pulled up in front of her place.

"That's a crazy kind of transportation for a woman her age," Jake said. "Does she really ride it everywhere she goes?"

"Rain or shine, it's the only way she can get wherever she needs to go," I said.

"She doesn't even *own* a car?"

"She hasn't had one for as long as I've known her, and that's been most of my life. Hattie has always been what you'd call a little flamboyant. I've never seen a woman go to such great lengths to dress in garish colors. She marches to the beat of her own drummer."

"I suppose that's one way of looking at it," Jake said as his stomach grumbled. "Should we forget about eating and go look for Max?"

"You poor thing. You're starving, aren't you?"

"I could eat," he said with a shrug, "but I've skipped meals before when I was working on a case, and I have a hunch it will happen again."

"Not on my watch, it won't. Stopping for fifteen minutes to grab a bite at the Boxcar isn't going to make any difference in the scheme of things."

"I don't know how you can say that," Jake replied. "I've seen a matter of seconds make the difference between life and death."

"I'm sure that you have, but I can't see that applying in this particular case. Come on. Let's go get something to eat."

"I'll do it for you, if you're really hungry," he said.

I looked over at him and saw that he was grinning. "Sure. *I'm* the only one who's hungry. If you don't want to eat, you could always just sit across the table from me and watch."

"I don't know," he answered as his eyes started twinkling. "That would be kind of rude. I'll probably order something too, but just to keep you company."

"I can't tell you how much I appreciate the sacrifices you make for me," I said with a laugh. At least we weren't very far from the Boxcar. Not only would it be good to get something to eat, but Trish, the diner's owner, might have heard something about Dusty's murder she could share with us. After all, not much in town occurred without her knowing at least *something* about it. Even if she didn't, though, we'd still get a hearty meal and a bit of lively conversation.

That much I knew that I could count on.

"What's new?" I asked Trish as we walked into the diner. The dining room had once been a train boxcar, hence the name. The kitchen was another boxcar, and Trish had been threatening for years to buy yet another to expand her operation. I liked things just the way they were at the moment. Not only was the place charming and cozy as it was, but it was also what I was used to, and there was something to be said for the familiar.

"Do you mean besides the fact that somebody bumped off Dusty Baxter?" she asked me. Her long blonde hair, pulled back in its ever-present ponytail, bobbed as she talked. "Do you really need anything else going on at the moment?"

"What have you heard?" I asked, lowering my voice in the hopes that she would follow suit. Trish didn't much care who overheard her, but I would be happier if we didn't include everyone there in our conversation if I had anything to say about it.

"Are you seriously asking *me*? *You're* the one who found the body, and I'll bet good money that you and your hubby are looking for his killer even as we speak. Suzanne, don't you ever get tired of stumbling over corpses?"

"More than you'll ever know," I said softly, reliving the moment despite my best wishes not to picture the crime scene ever again. "It was just awful."

Trish took a moment to think about what I said, and then she gave me an enveloping hug. We'd gone to school together, and besides Grace Gauge, she was just about my best friend ever, if I didn't count Momma and Jake. I knew that not everyone could say that their spouses and parents were also their friends, but I couldn't imagine living my life any other way.

"Can you ever forgive me? I don't always think before I shoot my mouth off. Obviously. How are you doing, darlin'?"

"I'm okay," I said.

"So then, you're *not* digging into Dusty's murder?"

"How can we not?" I asked her softly. "Finding the body like that kind of makes it our business, you know?"

She finally got the hint and lowered her voice to match mine. "Suzanne, is it true what they are saying?"

"I don't know," I said in all honesty. "What exactly are they saying?"

"That Emily's stuffed animals were found at the crime scene, and that there was blood everywhere, including on them. From what I've heard, she'll have to throw them away, things were so bad."

I knew better than just about anyone else about the condition of Cow, Spots, and Moose, but it wasn't my place to share everything I knew. Still, I could at least dispel one rumor. "There wasn't much blood at all, and what there was wasn't on the guys, at least as far as I could tell." I glanced over at Jake, who wasn't thrilled with me sharing so much of what I knew, but while I had promised to keep the police chief's confidence about staying silent about Spots holding the knife, I hadn't said anything about confirming or denying that they were even there. I knew that Jake wouldn't have said anything, but we were two different people, despite how close we were. Getting married hadn't stopped either one of us from having our own opinions, and they didn't *always* have to go hand in hand.

"That's a relief, anyway," Trish said. "I'm guessing you don't have much time to hang around gossiping with me, not if you're hot on the heels of a killer. The special today is excellent, and what makes it even better is the fact that there's no waiting. We were all missing our Thanksgiving feast here, so we decided to do a spread out of season."

"Turkey and all the fixings are *always* in season as far as I'm concerned," Jake said. "We'll take two, right, Suzanne?"

"Sure, but then what are you going to eat?" I asked, teasing him.

"So, should I bring two plates, or three?" Trish asked me.

"Surprise us," I said at the same time that Jake held up two fingers.

"Seriously. We just need one apiece," he said.

Trish glanced at me, and I pretended to be a little put out. "Fine, but if I'm still hungry, will you bring me another one after I finish with the first one?"

"If you're still hungry after polishing one of these plates, I'll pay for the second one myself," she said with a grin.

"Don't encourage her," Jake said with a grin. "Now she's going to do it just to prove that she can."

"I don't *need* any proof," Trish said. "I've seen her eat, remember? If she says she can eat two specials, I believe her."

"Okay, enough chitchat. Go fetch our food, woman," I said with a smile.

"You bet," she said. "Two teas with it?"

"That sounds great," I said.

After we took a table near the back, I pulled out my cell phone. Jake looked at me inquisitively. "Who are you calling?"

"I thought I'd put out a few feelers on where Max might be," I said. "Do you mind?"

"No, go right ahead."

I called a few people I thought might know my ex's whereabouts, but I hit three dead ends in a row.

"No luck?" Jake asked me as I put my phone away.

"Not yet, but I'm not ready to give up that easily."

As I looked around to see who else was eating at the Boxcar, I overheard some of our fellow townsfolk talking about the murder, which was no great surprise. After all, it was a big deal for a small town to lose one of its own to homicide. I started sampling the conversations, listening in when I thought it might be relevant. I'd mastered the art of eavesdropping over the years, so as Jake and I held an inane conversation about the weather, I listened in to bits and pieces of chatter.

Most of it was just idle speculation until I heard something that certainly caught my attention. "...screaming in his face that he wasn't going to get away with it, and not twenty-four hours later, the man's as dead as a doornail. That's a funny expression, isn't it? What's a doornail, and why on earth would it be dead, if it were never alive in the first place?"

"Actually, there's an interesting story to that," her companion said. "It dates back to the fourteenth century, and even William Shakespeare and Charles Dickens used the phrase."

"Charles Dickens wasn't born in the fourteenth century," the first woman said. "I wrote a history report on him in high school, and I still remember his birthday, February 7, 1812. It was the same date as my first boyfriend."

"You dated a boy born in 1812?" the woman asked her incredulously. "I knew that you'd been around awhile, but that's frankly unbelievable."

"February 7, not 1812," the other woman said with a mean bark to it.

"So then he was born after Dickens. Is that what you're saying?"

"Considerably. How did we get off on this tangent?"

"You were telling me about Hattie arguing with Dusty just before he died."

That was all I could take. I stood up and walked straight to the table, where Minerva Gant was talking to Jillian Moore. "Minerva, what were they fighting about?"

"Hello, Suzanne. I'm sorry, was our conversation bothering you? We'll try to keep it down from now on." Minerva had a wicked look in her eyes. It was clear that she was enjoying the attention and the power of knowing something that I didn't.

"Minerva, what were they arguing about?" I repeated.

"What's in it for me if I tell you?" she asked coyly.

I was about to tell her that I might let her live if she talked, but then I remembered Minerva's famous love of raspberry donuts. "How does half a dozen raspberry donuts sound tomorrow morning?"

"I don't know. A dozen sounds better," she said.

I wasn't about to quibble over six donuts. "Done. Now talk."

Jake had joined us, and he was clearly just as interested in her answer as I was. Minerva nodded, satisfied with our agreement. "It was over money."

"There has to be more to it than that. Think, Minerva. Otherwise your dozen raspberry-filled treats just got knocked down to two single glazed donuts."

Minerva clearly didn't like that, and she realized that playing any more games with me wasn't going to work. "I happened to be dozing in the sun when I heard Hattie call out to Dusty. They met in front of the bench by the clock, and if either one of them noticed me, I'll pay you a dollar each. Anyway, Hattie asked him where the first payment was, and Dusty acted as though she was speaking Latin. When she pushed him on it, he just shrugged and said, 'You never said when you wanted the money paid back, so I just figured I'd wait a few months."

"'That is a lie, and you know it!' That's what Hattie screamed at him as she poked him in the chest. 'You have until sunset tomorrow to pay me back in full, or else.' I couldn't believe how angry she was. I was afraid the poor dear was going to have a coronary on the spot."

"How did Dusty react to that?" I asked.

"He just laughed. Wow, Hattie didn't like that, let me tell you. She got kind of quiet, and when she spoke again, her words were like tiny little daggers."

After a very pregnant pause, I asked, "What did she say?"

Minerva's voice got low, and then she reported, "Hattie said, 'Or else means that you won't live to see another sunrise.' I tell you, I get chills now just thinking about it." After a moment, Minerva asked, "Am I back up to a dozen raspberry now?"

"Come by in the morning and you can collect," I said as Trish walked up with a tray laden with food and two drinks.

"Are you two eating here now?"

"No, we're going back to our own table," I said. As we did, I asked Jake softly, "What do you think of that?"

"I think we have more to talk to Hattie about now than we did before," he said. As we sat down, Trish put the plates laden with turkey, dressing, mashed potatoes, sweet potatoes, green beans, cranberry sauce, and rolls in front of us. She'd been right.

I doubted I'd be able to eat one of these monsters, no matter how delicious it looked, let alone two.

"If you need anything, just whistle. You know how to whistle, don't you?" she asked us, giving us her best Lauren Bacall impression.

"You bet," Jake said, putting two fingers in his mouth and emitting a shrill sound that stopped everything in the diner.

"Okay, you know how," Trish said as she looked around and added in a loud voice, "That was a test of the April Springs Emergency Broadcast system. It was only a test. Had it been a real emergency, you would have seen me running for the nearest exit. Everybody can go back to their food now."

There were several chuckles, but I noticed a few folks give Jake an odd look. That was okay by me. I'd been getting odd looks my entire life, and it suited me to finally be married to someone who merited them as well.

"This is amazing," I said after I took the first bite. The ladies in back had outdone themselves, and I saw that Jake was enjoying his every bit as much as I was savoring mine. "Should we talk about what we just heard?" I asked him between morsels.

"Let's wait until we're outside," Jake said. "This meal is so good, I kind of feel like it deserves our complete attention."

I knew it had to be good if Jake was willing to put our investigation on hold, but I didn't disagree with the sentiment at all. Every bite was better than the last, and I suddenly realized that I'd managed to eat everything Trish had brought me after all.

Jake grinned at me when he saw that I had polished off my plate. "Are you ready for Round Two, Suzanne?"

"You're kidding, right? I'm going to be lucky if I don't fall asleep before we get back to the Jeep."

"Then let's pay and get out of here. I know we need to look

for Max, but after what Minerva told us, I really want to speak with Hattie again."

"I'm with you there," I said as I paid Trish, being careful not to overtip her. She hated getting more than she thought she deserved almost as much as she disliked getting less.

Once we were outside, I stretched in the fading sunlight. "I just hope Hattie is back home."

"I can tell you without a doubt that she's not," Jake said.

"How could you possibly know that?" I asked him.

My husband pointed over my shoulder toward the donut shop, which was close to the Boxcar Grill, a fact that I was more than a little happy about most days, especially when I was craving some of Trish's delightful fare.

"Because she's right there, slipping a note under the door of Donut Hearts."

CHAPTER 11

"H EY, HATTIE. WHAT ARE YOU up to?" I asked as we walked over to Donut Hearts and stood behind her. She was still trying her best to get a note under the door, but since I'd had it redone after a storm had demolished most of the front of the building, it was a much tighter fit than it had been before.

"Hello. There you are," she said, catching her breath. Had she really been struggling that hard to get the folded paper through the slit, or was she tired for another reason? Her tricycle was parked on the sidewalk in front of Donut Hearts, but I doubted that riding it around town had worn her out. "I need you both to stop bothering me!"

"Let me get this straight. You're standing in front of *my* donut shop trying to leave *me* a note, and you believe that *I'm* the one bothering *you*?" I asked her, amused by her indignation.

"Millie Farnsworth told me you were snooping around my cottage when I wasn't home earlier," she said, looking triumphant at catching us in the act of something she thought we shouldn't have been doing. "Don't bother denying it."

"We wouldn't dream of it," I said. "We were indeed there. I'm glad you came by. You saved us another trip to your place."

"Suzanne, are you growing deaf? I just told you that I didn't want to speak with you anymore." She looked thoroughly confused by my nonresponse.

"And yet here we stand, all having a nice little chat. Hattie, we need to talk about Dusty Baxter," I said, watching her carefully as I said the dead man's name.

"What about him?" she asked, her eyes narrowing to two slits. "I was under the impression you were trying to find Emily's stuffed animals."

"We found them," I said.

"Well, bully for you. If you found them, then why exactly are you asking me about Dusty? I rue the fact that I spoke with you in the first place, and if there's anything I'd like to talk about less than three missing stuffed animals, it's Dusty Baxter."

"You haven't heard the news, have you?" Jake asked her.

She rolled her eyes before she answered. "I'm sure I don't know what you're talking about. What is this supposed news?"

It was as unconvincing as the last performance of hers I'd seen. "Are you saying you've been tooling around town on your trike and no one has stopped you with the news about him?" It was beyond belief that she didn't already know.

"That's exactly what I'm saying. A few folks tried to flag me down, but I didn't have time to stop. I'm a busy woman with things to do. Now I'll ask you one more time, and then I'm finished with this conversation, and with you. What is this so-called news?"

"Dusty's dead, Hattie," I said.

Again, she overplayed her response. It was obvious to me that she was lying about knowing Dusty's fate. I just didn't understand why yet. "What? That's impossible! Why, I saw him just last night!"

"We know," Jake said. "It sounds as though you two had quite an argument near the clock on Town Square."

"So, she wasn't sleeping after all," Hattie mumbled under her breath. "I should have known the old bat was faking it."

"It's refreshing that you're not trying to deny it," I said. "You threatened him, didn't you?"

Hattie held up her hands as though she were warding off a blow. "Hold on now. You've got it all wrong. I asked for the repayment of a small loan I made him, and when he balked, I may have gotten a little carried away in my reaction, but I'm just a harmless old woman. I wouldn't hurt anyone."

"It's funny, but you never asked us how he died," I said.

"I just assumed he was shot. The world is full of too many firearms, if you ask me."

"As a matter of fact," Jake said, "he was stabbed to death."

"Oh. That's dreadful. I still don't know what it has to do with me." Again, she was acting more in line with a play than a real-life reaction.

"Hattie, you had an argument with a murder victim the night before he was slain, and you were heard threatening to end him. Why *wouldn't* we want to speak with you about it?" This woman was pushing me more than I could tolerate.

"Neither one of you is a member of any police force that I know of, so what concern is it of yours?" Hattie asked. "I don't have to stand here and answer questions that are none of your business."

"That's perfectly true," Jake said in a calm voice. "I'm sure the police will be along shortly to speak with you instead."

Hattie acted as though that thought had never even occurred to her. "I'm not quite sure why you're making so much of this. After all, it was all perfectly innocent."

"Then help us help you," I said. "We can be powerful allies." I wasn't sure why I'd just said that, though it was true. Jake and I were good allies and even worse foes.

Hattie looked for a moment as though she was going to say something in response to my offer when I noticed a car drive up in my peripheral vision.

It was the chief of police, and he didn't look particularly happy with *any* of us.

"There you are," Chief Grant said to Hattie once he got out and approached the three of us. "I've been looking for you for the past hour."

She blanched at the news. "I don't care what you might think. I didn't kill that man!"

"So, you already know about Dusty," the police chief said, frowning at me for a second. "I suppose that was unavoidable, given the circumstances. Do you have a second to talk about it?"

"Actually, I'm rather late for an appointment, but I could probably squeeze you in sometime tomorrow," Hattie said as she put a hand on her tricycle handlebar.

"I'm afraid that's not going to work for me," the chief said. "Why don't we take care of it right now, and that way I won't have to bother you tomorrow?"

"It's getting dark," Hattie said, clearly trying to stall him again. "I hate riding my tricycle after the sun goes down. It's much too dangerous."

"I'll see that it gets home safely, and when we're finished, I'll drive you back to your cottage myself. How does that sound?"

"Impossible," Hattie said. "I won't hear of it. No one, and I mean no one touches my transportation other than me. If you want to arrest me, then go right ahead and be my guest, but I'm riding it straight home this very instant."

The chief looked as though he was considering locking her up just to prove a point, but after a moment, he relented. It might have had something to do with the crowd we were amassing, including Ray Blake, the newspaper editor, who happened to have his camera phone at the ready to record anything that might be of interest to his readers. "Fine. I'll follow you home in my squad car, and we can speak there."

Hattie looked as though she wanted to protest further, but evidently she knew when she'd reached the end of her excuses. "I don't see how that could possibly work. I ride much slower than you drive, Chief."

"I don't think anyone's going to complain. Think of it as a police escort. After all, we wouldn't want anything to happen to you along the way, now would we?"

Hattie shook her head and finally mounted her tricycle, forgetting all about us for the moment.

As she rode away, the chief asked us, "Did you get anything out of her?"

"Out of *her*? No," I said, being careful with my wording. I wasn't about to lie to him, but I wasn't sure how much I should volunteer, either.

Jake clearly had other ideas. "There's something you need to know. Hattie had a fight with Dusty last night. He owed her money, and he was reluctant to pay it back promptly. Evidently Hattie took exception to that, and she threatened to kill him."

"How did you happen to come across that information?" the chief asked my husband. I couldn't tell from his reaction whether he knew about it or not.

"Minerva Gant overheard the whole thing. I'd talk to her if I were you."

"I already have," the chief said as he nodded. "She came by my office ten minutes ago. Thanks for sharing, Jake."

"I was going to tell you eventually," I protested.

Both men looked at me with raised eyebrows.

"Well, I was. Shouldn't you be on your way, Chief? It looks as though Hattie is breaking her best speed record on that thing." They both looked after the older actress and saw that I wasn't lying. She was really flying on that tricycle. If I hadn't seen it with my own eyes, I never would have believed that she could pedal that fast.

"You're right. I'd better go," he said as he headed to his

cruiser. I half expected him to use the siren and flashing lights, but he chose to do neither.

Once he was gone, I asked Jake, "Was that a trap the chief just set for us?"

"He wanted to know if he could trust us," my husband said. "I had to tell him, Suzanne."

"I know that. I also realize that I should have said something myself. Do you think he's angry with me?"

"No more than usual when we're meddling in his business," Jake said. "As long as one of us said something, we're fine."

"Then I'm glad that it was you. You didn't mention Emily's news."

He nodded. "I was going to, but he left before I got the chance."

"Jake, we agreed to let her tell him herself," I scolded him.

"Hang on. I was going to mention that he should speak with her as soon as possible. I wasn't going to tell him why, Suzanne."

"Then I apologize," I answered contritely.

"And I accept," he replied with a grin.

"I don't know what I did to deserve you, but I'm glad that I did," I said as my cell phone rang. "Hang on. I need to take this."

"Is it Grace or your mother?" he asked me as he smiled.

"It *might* be someone else," I said.

"Sure, but what are the odds?"

It turned out that they were actually pretty good, since it was the mayor on the line. I'd called George Morris earlier about Max, but he hadn't known anything at the time. George had helped me with some of my earliest cases, but I didn't like to consult with him anymore. Not only did I not want to interfere with his ability to be our mayor, but I'd inadvertently put his life in jeopardy once, and there was no way I could ever allow that to happen again.

"Hey, George," I said as I grinned at my husband. "What's up?"

"Are you still looking for Max?" the mayor asked, dispensing with small talk altogether.

"I am. What have you got for me?"

"I might know where he is," George said. "The thing is, if you go without me, it might spook him. Jake is with you, right?"

"He's standing right here. Why, do you need to speak with him?"

"No, I just wanted to make sure you weren't going to face Max alone if you decide not to let me tag along," the mayor said.

"George, I don't have anything to fear from Max." The notion was patently absurd. We'd had our differences over the years, but there had never been even the slightest hint of violence on my ex's part toward me. I wasn't even sure he was capable of it under the most extreme provocation.

"Suzanne, Dusty Baxter is dead, and I'm pretty sure it wasn't suicide."

"No, he was clearly murdered," I said, still puzzled as to why he thought Max might have something to do with it.

Unless he knew something I didn't. "You were the one, weren't you?" I asked him as the pieces all started to fall into place.

"The one what?" he asked. Now it was his turn to be confused.

"You walked in on Dusty and Emily last night," I said.

"Dusty and Emily Hargraves were having a fling? You're kidding." There was no way George was faking his stunned reaction.

Wow, had I ever gotten that wrong. I had to end that particular rumor, and fast. "No. They weren't having a fling. Dusty and Emily *were* together at the newsstand last night, but it wasn't because of an affair. They had an argument, not a tryst."

"But they dated before Max came into the picture, didn't they?" he asked me.

94

"Yes, but that's been over for a while," I said.

"Maybe so, but did Max realize what was going on? He's the jealous type these days. If he saw Emily with Dusty, he might act first and ask questions later," George said.

"Not Max," I said, though a little doubt was beginning to creep into my mind. Was it possible that Max had indeed had a confrontation with Dusty about Emily after he'd tried to assault Emily? "George, let's keep this conversation between the two of us, okay?"

"I suppose we could do that," the mayor said, "on one condition."

"What's that?" I asked, wondering what George was going to ask for. I knew he wouldn't be bought off with a dozen donuts; that was for sure.

"I told you a minute ago. I want in," George said plainly.

"In on what?" I asked, not getting what he was going for at all.

"The investigation," he explained.

That was exactly what I was trying to avoid, but how could I say it without hurting his feelings? "Jake and I are already working together on this. We can't have too many investigators, or we'll tip our hand to the killer too soon."

"I'm not asking to be the lead detective, but I want to play a part, no matter how small it might be. Suzanne, once upon a time I was a very good cop. Use me."

"May I at least speak with Jake about it first?" I asked, trying to buy a little time.

"Sure. Do you want me to hold?"

"I need a minute," I said. "I'll call you right back."

He just laughed. "I was just teasing you," the mayor replied. "But don't take too long."

"I promise," I said.

Once I hung up, I realized that George had craftily avoided

giving me the lead he'd been calling about. It was clear that I was going to have to give in to his request to get the information I needed. I wasn't sure I cared for his tactics, but if our roles had been reversed, I couldn't say that I wouldn't have done the exact same thing.

But first I needed to speak with Jake.

"That was George on the phone, not Momma and not Grace," I said.

"I gathered as much. What's going on, Suzanne? I got the gist of it from your end right up until the end. What does the mayor want from you?"

I explained, "George wants to be part of our investigation." Before Jake could protest, I added, "He doesn't want to take the lead. He just wants to help."

"That sounds good to me. He's got good instincts," Jake said.

"You're seriously okay with this?" I asked him.

"I don't see that we have much choice. Did he say that he knew where Max was?"

"I'm going to call him right back and find out," I said as I pulled my cell phone out of my pocket and made the call.

CHAPTER 12

"Wow, THAT WAS FAST," GEORGE said when he answered my call on the first ring.

"You didn't give me much choice, did you?" I asked. "We've discussed it, and we accept your demand."

There was a momentary pause on the other end of the line, and then the mayor said, "Suzanne, I wasn't trying to blackmail you into letting me help you."

"That's funny, because that's sure how it felt on this end," I answered, keeping my voice light as I said it. I never would have dreamed of texting something like that. I felt that all nuance went out the window when I started texting, and it had gotten me into trouble on more than one occasion.

"I've changed my mind," George said.

"After all that, you're not going to tell us where Max is? Why are you protecting him, Mr. Mayor? You don't think he's guilty, do you?"

"I was a cop too long to try to worry about someone's guilt or innocence. All I was ever after was fact. If I couldn't prove something, it might as well not have happened, at least as far as I was concerned."

"Then why are you shielding him?"

Jake looked at me curiously, but I didn't answer. After I held up one finger to ask him for his indulgence for a little while longer, I asked, "George? Are you still there?"

"Of course I'm still here. I'm not fool enough to hang up on you. What I meant to say was that I'll help you without any tit for tat on your part. If you don't want me to pitch in, I'm too proud to beg or extort my way into the inner circle."

Evidently I'd taken my teasing a little too far. "George, Jake and I would be honored to have your help on this case. The only reason, and I mean the only one, we weren't sure was that we didn't want to make things tough for you in your day job."

"There are worse things than losing an election," the mayor said.

"Coming from the incumbent, that's an odd thing to hear."

"The truth of the matter is that I'd rather lose a dozen elections than a good friend," he said.

The old dear was actually telling me how he felt about me! It warmed my heart to hear it, especially since it was so out of character for George to express his emotions like that. I was about to say as much when he added, "Besides, I don't have many friends who used to be cops, let alone state police inspectors."

Wow, had I misread that! I took a few deep breaths to collect myself before I heard George laughing on the other end. "What's so funny?"

"Suzanne, sometimes it's almost too easy tweaking your nose. Of course I meant you! Now let's knock this nonsense off and get down to business. Answer me one more time, and it had better be the truth. Do you and Jake mind if I tag along with you this evening?"

"We'd love to have you," I said.

Jake was just shaking his head, giving up on trying to follow our conversation from my end alone. That was okay with me. I'd known the mayor a lot longer than I'd known my husband, and George and I had an odd relationship, anyway.

"Fair enough. You remember where my cabin on the lake is, don't you?"

"I fell into the water the last time I was there," I said. "That's a little hard to forget."

"I thought you claimed you were pushed," George asked.

"I'm tired of arguing with the entire town about it, but Timmy Braswell knows what he did," I said, remembering the little scamp throwing out an arm as he ran past me that day to shove me into the drink.

"Okay. Max should be there about now. He swung by two minutes before I called you and got my key."

"You're hiding him out yourself?" I asked loud enough to make Jake feel the need to shush me.

"I offered him a place to collect himself," the mayor said. "He's pretty torn up about Emily."

"Why is that?" I asked. Jake was begging for information at that point, but I couldn't exactly put the mayor on speakerphone.

"He saw her with Dusty at the newsstand last night. I told you that it wasn't me."

"You didn't mention that before," I said, chiding him a little for withholding information. Some folks would have thought it took a lot of nerve for me to be upset about what I'd been doing to the police chief myself, but that was like comparing apples and oranges, at least as far as I was concerned.

"I just found out myself," he said. "I'm telling you, he was devastated by the thought of her cheating on him."

"Emily has too much class to do that, and what's more, he should know that by now," I said, though that was exactly what my ex-husband had done to me.

"That's what I told him."

"What did he say?"

"He mumbled something about payback being a bear, past sins coming back to bite him on the rear end, and something about birds coming home to roost, and then he took off. Do you want to pick me up, or should we all just meet at the cabin?"

"I don't want Max to see us coming," I said.

"Wait for me at the top of the hill," he said. "We can walk down together."

"Okay, but if you get there before we do, you need to be the one who waits for us," I admonished him.

"Right back at you," he said, his voice sounding younger than it had in years. He was clearly enjoying the prospect of being in on the chase again.

After we hung up, Jake said, "That was the world's longest conversation I was never a part of. Do you mind catching me up?"

"I'd love to, but can we do it while we're driving? Max is at George's cabin at the lake."

"I'm fine with talking and riding at the same time," Jake said. As we got into the Jeep and started driving in the darkness toward the cabin, I had to stifle a yawn. I was already up past my bedtime, but tonight I was just going to have to tough it out. After all, just because I had a quirky schedule didn't mean that the rest of the world stopped when I had to go to bed. I'd pulled late-nighters before, and I knew that if I kept investigating murder, it would happen again.

Once we were on the road, I explained everything to Jake. "Max is the one who walked in on Dusty just as he was cornering Emily. He misread the situation and took off. At the moment, he's at the mayor's cabin on the lake licking his wounds, so if we're lucky, we'll catch him off guard."

"You're going to hate what I'm about to say, but we really should call Chief Grant," Jake said after a moment of staring out the Jeep window.

"I admire your desire to keep the police up to speed on things, but do me a favor and wait. I really need to speak with Max first and find out for myself if he might have committed murder."

"Suzanne, we can't let our emotions rule us."

"Ordinarily I'd agree with that, but this is different. No matter how badly he hurt me, once upon a time we were married. I love you with all my heart, but I can't ignore the life I led before we met."

"I'm not asking you to do that," Jake said.

"So you'll wait?"

After a few more seconds, Jake nodded. "After we're finished with him, we'll call the police chief. Tell you what. We can do better than that. We'll convince Max that he needs to call the chief himself. It will go a lot easier on him if he goes in willingly."

"Jake, he's not even a suspect in Dusty's murder as far as the police are concerned."

"So far, but how long do you think that's going to last once Chief Grant finds out that Max caught Emily and Dusty together in a compromising position the night before the murder?"

"I'd say not more than two or three seconds," I admitted. "That doesn't mean that he's guilty, though."

"Let's just see what he has to say for himself once we talk to him," Jake said as I continued to drive to the lake. "I keep wondering how the mayor of April Springs who used to be a cop can afford a house on the lake."

"You've never been there before, have you?" I asked. The last time I'd been there myself was when I'd been dropped into the water, and that was long before I met Jake.

"No, I haven't had the pleasure. Is it nice?"

"I'm sure the mice and raccoons just love it there," I said with a grin. "They must, since they keep getting in and setting up house. Why they wouldn't rather be outside is beyond me. The place is in pretty bad need of a major renovation."

"Still, the property must be worth a fortune alone," Jake said. "How did the mayor acquire it? From what I've heard about George, he's never had a lot of money. I'm not even going to think about the possibility that he was ever on someone else's payroll."

"George? A dirty cop? No way. I'd bet my life on that. When he was on the force, he used to love to play poker, though. The way he tells the story, one night a buddy of his thought he had a winning hand, but he was out of cash. George did his best to convince him to fold his hand, but the guy thought he was bluffing. This guy offered the deed to his property, which believe me, wasn't worth nearly as much back then as it must be now. George kept protesting, but finally, the guy wouldn't shut up, so he took him up on his offer. George won the hand, and the rest is April Springs history."

"If the place is such a dump, why would Max even want to stay there?" Jake asked as we began to near the mayor's property.

"I have to give him credit for coming up with the idea. I thought I knew all of Max's hiding places, but George's cabin never even occurred to me. There's the mayor now," I said as I flashed my headlights before turning them off and parking beside him.

"I can't believe my banged-up old pickup truck beat your brand-new Jeep," George said with a grin as he shook my husband's hand.

"You had a head start," I chided him as Jake got a heavy police flashlight out of the back of my Jeep. It amused me to see that George had one that was identical to the one my husband was now carrying. I felt as though I'd forgotten something, since I was the only one empty-handed. "I should warn you both, Max isn't going to be too happy to see any of us. Is there any chance you'll let me go in first and speak with him alone?"

I was fearful for a moment that the resounding nos shouted out would alert everyone on the lake that we were there.

"I just thought I'd ask," I said. "At least let me do the talking."

The mayor nodded, most likely just happy to be there, but Jake wasn't so pliable. "Suzanne, I know you and Max have this bond you keep telling me about, but I'm afraid you have a soft spot when it comes to your ex-husband. You have a tendency to let him off the hook, and don't bother trying to deny it."

I saw George's eyes go wide as he took a step back to get out of the line of fire, but instead of reacting instantly as was my nature most of the time, I thought about what Jake said. Was it true that I cut Max too much slack? After the divorce, I'd barely spoken to him for years, and if I'd seen him walking down the other side of the street while I was driving, I'd have had to fight the temptation to run him down. That had changed though, and a great deal of it had to do with Emily Hargraves. Being with her had somehow civilized him, softened him to the point where I didn't hate him anymore, and then I didn't mind being around him, and finally, much to my astonishment, we'd become friends. Maybe Jake was right. "Okay, I can see why you'd say that, but trust me, if he killed Dusty Baxter, nobody wants to see him pay for the crime more than I do." I glanced over at the mayor, who was now staring at me with wide-open astonishment. "What are you looking at?" I asked curtly.

"Me? Nothing. Nothing at all."

He so studiously avoided my glaring gaze that I couldn't help bursting out laughing. "Are you two ready?"

"Lead the way," Jake said. "We'll be right behind you."

As we made our way down the path, I nearly stumbled two or three times, since both lights were behind me. "As much as

I appreciate the offer, one of you really should lead the way. Otherwise I'm probably just going to end up in the lake again."

Jake handed me his flashlight. "Keep going. You're doing fine," he said.

"Thanks," I replied as I played the light down on the path. There were tree roots and rocks all over the place, and it was a wonder anyone made it down it at all without breaking their necks somewhere along the way.

Once we were close to the door, the porch light put out enough illumination so that I could see the last bit of walkway, so I shut my flashlight off, and George did the same thing.

I was still out of the porch light's direct vicinity when I heard an oddly dangerous-sounding voice from the porch say, "One more step and I'll shoot you right where you stand."

CHAPTER 13

"I'T'S JUST US, MAX!" I said loudly into the darkness. "Don't shoot!"

"Suzanne, is that you? What are you doing out here?" Max asked, clearly perplexed by my presence.

"*I* brought her," the mayor said.

"Come on, George. Seriously?"

"I'm here, too, so you'd better have more than two bullets if you want to get all of us," Jake answered as well.

"I'm not armed," Max explained.

"No kidding," Jake answered. "I've got to admit that you sounded pretty convincing just then, though."

"Hey, I'm an actor. It's what I do," he said with more than a little pride in his voice. "What are you all doing here? I don't want to talk to anybody."

The three of us started walking toward the light, and as we climbed the porch steps, Jake said, "That's too bad, because we need to talk to you."

"Let me guess. It's about Dusty, isn't it?" he asked as we joined him.

"Do you really want to do this out here?" I asked. "You should invite us in."

"It's not my place to decide who comes in and who doesn't," Max said.

"That's true enough," the mayor said as he walked past Max into his cabin. "Are you all coming?"

For a second I thought Max might make a run for it, but Jake took one slight step sideways, effectively blocking his way off the porch.

I heard my ex-husband let out a sigh. "Fine."

"After you," Jake said.

"I'm not going anywhere," Max protested.

"Max, that's a dangerous game you just played. If you claim to be armed, you'd better have a weapon on you and be ready to fire. What if I'd called your bluff?"

"What were you going to do, shoot me? You're not armed, either."

Jake didn't have to say a word. All he had to do was raise his eyebrows and purse his lips.

"Well, it seemed like a good idea at the time," Max said.

"Come on. Let's not do this out here on the front porch. Sound carries on the water. We don't know who might be listening in."

"There's nobody within ten miles of us," Max said. "Why do you think I wanted to stay out here awhile?" Max walked inside, with Jake and me close on his heels. I had to admit that the place was a bit cozier than the last time I'd seen it.

"Mr. Mayor, have you been having help decorating the cabin?" I asked him. "Say, a woman, by any chance?"

George actually blushed a little. "It's not really important at the moment, is it? We're not exactly here to talk about interior design." Mayor Morris then turned to my ex-husband and asked, "Max, what have you gotten yourself into?"

"Nothing! I swear I didn't kill Dusty!"

"Then why are you out here hiding by yourself at the lake?" I asked him.

"I needed some time to sort some things out," he said, pouting.

"You're an idiot. You know that, don't you?" I asked him.

My words stung him; that much was clear by the way he recoiled. I doubted he would have flinched more if I'd actually slapped him with an open hand. "That's kind of harsh, don't you think?"

"Did you honestly think for one second that Emily Hargraves would cheat on you with Dusty Baxter? She loves you, though I can't for the life of me figure out why. You saw them together, you panicked, and you ran, didn't you?"

"Yes," Max admitted, looking as though he'd just lost his best friend. "I decided not to do the commercial after all, so I flew back home to surprise Emily. When I walked into the newsstand, I saw him pressed against her, and I had to get out of there."

"*You* decided not to do it, or did they fire you?" the mayor asked him.

"Let's just say that it was a mutual decision. I quit over creative differences with the director at the same time he decided to go in another direction. It happens more often than you might think," Max said, which was his typical excuse when he got fired in the past.

"I don't care why you came back. Why didn't you confront Emily and Dusty right then and there?" Jake asked. "That's what *I* would have done."

"We're not the same," Max said.

"I thank my blessings every day for that," I said, "but it makes you look guilty, Max, can't you see that? You hiding here is bad for everyone who cares about you, most of all Emily. She was fighting Dusty's advances off. If you'd gone all the way inside, you would have known that. The truth is, you should have known it anyway. Where were you at the time of the murder?" I told him the time frame, but he just shook his head.

"I have no idea. I started drinking last night after what I thought I saw, and I didn't wake up until this afternoon. I didn't even know Dusty was dead until the mayor here told me," he said dejectedly.

"I don't suppose anyone got drunk *with* you, did they?" Jake asked him.

"No. I was alone." In a voice that softened immediately, he asked, "How's Emily doing?"

"How would you think she was doing? After all, she's a suspect, too," the mayor said. "Plus, I'm sure she's wondering why her fiancé decided to desert her when she needed him the most."

"She didn't kill him, either!" Max shouted as he shot off the chair where he'd been sitting. "I can't believe the cops would ever suspect her! She's innocent!"

"And you can prove that how, exactly?" Jake asked him calmly, ignoring my ex-husband's vehement reaction.

Max stormed toward the door. "I can't, but I'm not going to let that stop me from helping her. Is she actually under arrest?"

"Not the last we heard," I said. "Max, I can appreciate your impulse to go storming off in her defense, but we're not finished here yet."

"You might not be, but I am," Max said as he pulled the cabin door open.

I heard the shot almost immediately as Max fell down like a discarded rag doll onto the floor.

CHAPTER 14

"MAX!" I SCREAMED AS BOTH Jake and George sprang into action the split second they heard the bullet hit something against the far wall with a resounding ring. Both men pulled out their weapons with practiced ease. A moment later, Jake slammed the heavy wooden door shut with his foot as George turned out the single inside light that had been on. As the mayor was getting the porch light as well, I rushed to Max's side.

"How bad is it?" I asked him as I knelt close to his face.

"I've been better," he said. "I hit my head pretty hard when I fell," he complained as he sat up and rubbed the back of his head.

"But you weren't shot?" I asked.

"No, they missed me," he said with a grimace as he started to stand. "Was it my imagination just then, or were you disappointed by the news?"

"Don't stand up," I said as I turned to my husband. "What do we do, Jake?"

"I just tried calling the chief, but I couldn't get a cell phone signal."

"It's hit or miss out here," George apologized. "What's our plan?"

"Our *plan*?" I asked, trying to keep my voice from hysteria. "There's no plan! We stay right where we are."

"First of all, that's a plan itself," George said.

"Do you really want to quibble with me about my word choice right now?" I asked him.

"Suzanne, if we stay here, we're sitting ducks," the mayor said, "and what's more, your husband knows it, too. We can't just wait for something to happen."

I knew he had a point, but I didn't have to like it. "How about shooting into the air to let whoever just shot at us know that we're armed, too?"

"It's too dangerous," Jake said. Enough moonlight peeked in through the window that I could see him shake his head. "I'm not taking the chance of hurting someone who has nothing to do with this. George, you stay here and I'll go do some recon."

"That's not happening, my friend," the mayor said. "We go together, or neither one of us goes."

"I don't mind staying behind. You know, just in case they try to break in," Max said lamely.

Both men ignored him.

"Okay then," Max said as he leaned back against a chair, rubbing his head. "How about if I let you two lawmen decide what happens next, and I'll just sit here nursing my throbbing skull?"

"Max, would you kindly shut up?" I asked without even glancing in his direction. "Jake, George is right. You shouldn't go out there alone."

"You haven't thought this through, Suzanne. What if whoever is out there is waiting for exactly that? If George and I leave you two here unarmed, you'll be vulnerable."

"I'm sitting right here, you know," Max said dryly.

Jake gave him a withering glance. "What are you going to do if someone comes rushing in with guns blazing? Threaten them? Sorry, but it's not happening."

Max finally decided to take my advice and keep his mouth shut after all.

"Why don't we all just take a breath?" I suggested. "There's no real immediate need to rush out into the darkness and confront whoever is out there, is there?"

"We aren't rushing anywhere, at least not yet," Jake said.

"Can we at least turn one of the little table lamps on? The dark is just making things creepier than they have to be. I can barely see with just the moonlight," Max protested. So much for heeding my advice to stay quiet and keep out of it.

"We can't do that," Jake explained. "We need to let our vision get accustomed to the low level of light. There's enough moonlight to see where we're going, so at least that's something."

"Listen to that," I said suddenly as I heard a car start up the hill from the cabin. "Is that what I think it is?"

"Probably," Jake said as he moved toward the door. "I'll go check it out. Alone," he added as he looked at George. "You're going to stay here, right?"

"Right," George said, though he was clearly unhappy about it.

Jake kissed me before he left, and then he whispered softly in my ear, "Don't worry about me. I'll be back in a second."

"Make sure of it," I said.

"Get away from the line of fire," he told Max in a much harsher tone of voice. "When I open this door, I don't want anyone to be in the shooter's line of sight, just in case they are still out there."

"We heard the car start up," Max protested. "Clearly whoever shot at us circled around, headed up the hill, and drove off."

"It's fine with me if you stay right where you are and hope that you are right," Jake said. "Suzanne, would you mind going over to the kitchen area?"

I moved without any more urging, but I didn't even try to get Max to abandon his position. If he wanted to take a chance that the shooter was waiting for another opportunity to get him, it was going to be entirely on his head, as sore as it might be at the moment from hitting the floor when he'd dived to get out of the line of fire.

After a moment, Max moved as well.

George moved to one side of the door. "At least let me cover you."

"Thanks," Jake said. He took a deep breath, and then he opened the door quietly with such gentle movements that if there hadn't been a sudden crouching darkness in the opening, I might not even have known that he was leaving. Going low, Jake snuck out of the cabin while George crouched down himself, his weapon out and ready to shoot at the slightest provocation.

There was no reason for him to fire his weapon, though.

"Shouldn't you close that door now that he's gone?" Max asked in a whisper, his voice clearly on edge because of the open exposure.

"No," George said just as softly. It amazed me how each man could convey so much emotion in whisper form. "Jake might need to get back inside in a hurry."

That sent a thousand dire thoughts racing through my mind. It felt like an hour while we waited for him to return, with each second frozen in time before moving on to the next.

Finally, even though I was sure it was imagination, I heard the voice I loved so much from the other side of the doorway. "It's me," Jake said loudly. The need for stealth was clearly past.

George's tension dispelled instantly as Jake walked in standing tall.

"You can turn on the lights," Jake instructed him. "Whoever took that shot is gone."

"If it's all the same to you, I'd still like to leave the lights off for a while," Max said.

Jake responded by turning on the nearest light, nearly

blinding me in the process. When he saw me flinch, he said, "Sorry about that."

"It's fine. I'm just glad that you're okay."

"It's all good," he said as he moved to the back wall directly in line with the door.

"What are you looking for?" Max asked him.

"The bullet that sent you diving for cover," Jake said as he studied the knotted pine paneling. "If we get lucky, we'll get something to compare later with ballistics."

"Unfortunately, that's not going to happen," George said as he held up a cast iron pan, one of many old relics decorating the wall. There was a dent in the cookware but no sign of any bullet. "I figured the bullet would either shatter the iron or punch its way straight through."

"It looks like it ricocheted back at the shooter instead," Jake said. "It's a shame it didn't hit whoever fired it in the first place. There would have been some nice poetic justice to that."

The comment was a part of my husband's darker side, one that he'd had to cultivate as a state police investigator, but I couldn't fault his argument. After all, someone had tried to kill one of us, probably Max. I didn't want them to die from the effort, but if they'd gotten nicked in the process by their own bullet in a ricochet, it would have served them right.

"So what do we do now?" Max asked.

"We get out of here and head straight for the police chief's office," Jake said.

"That would kind of ruin the point for me coming out here," Max said. "I didn't want to run into him and have to answer a thousand questions about Dusty and about what I saw last night, or what I thought I saw."

"Sorry, but that's not an option anymore." Jake looked at me and asked, "Do you mind driving back to the police station alone?"

"How are you going to get there?" I asked, though I had a sneaking suspicion that I knew the answer to my question before I even asked it.

"Max here is going to give me a ride, aren't you, Max?" Jake asked with a smile.

My ex-husband looked as though he'd rather kiss a skunk on the lips, but he nodded anyway. "Sure, I don't mind. You don't trust me, do you?"

"No, not entirely," Jake said. He was being kind at that, and what's more, everyone in that cabin knew it.

"I'm guessing it's more like not at all, but you know what? I can live with that," Max said. "Let's get this over with."

As we shut the cabin door and walked back up the hill together, I couldn't help but notice in the beam of my flashlight that George's limp, something he'd lived with since I'd gotten him into a dangerous situation with a killer, was noticeably better. "You've got a spring in your step tonight. You know that, don't you?"

"What can I say? Some nights it's just good to be alive," he said, clearly enjoying our little excursion, even *with* the shooting. Heck, as far as I knew, that might have been an added bonus for him.

"I'd say that goes for all of the nights," Max said.

For some reason that struck us all as funny, whether it was actually amusing or we were just getting over just how badly things could have gone for us. We all started laughing, and even Max joined in.

Once we were at the top of the hill in the parking area for George's cabin, the two former cops took their flashlights and studied the ground carefully around them.

George pointed to a dark patch. "Is that antifreeze, by any chance?"

Jake touched a finger to the dirt, smelled it, and then, to my horror, he sampled it.

"Jake, don't taste that! It's poison!" I shouted.

"Relax, Suzanne. It's just soda. Someone emptied out their can." He scanned the surrounding area, but he couldn't find the can itself.

"Oh, well. It was worth a shot," he said. "Let's go, folks. It's already late, and Suzanne is up way past her bedtime."

I glanced at my watch and saw that I was already two hours behind my usual sleep schedule, but tonight was going to have to be an exception. I knew that I could call Emma and Sharon to sub for me, but I was only running Donut Hearts five days a week as it was, and I was very protective of those days. "Don't worry about me. I'll be fine."

"Still, we need to get going," Jake said. "Are you good to drive, Max, or do you want to give me the keys?"

"I can manage just fine," Max said.

As they got into Max's older vehicle, George asked me, "Suzanne, do you mind if I leave my truck here and ride into town with you?"

"No, of course not, but how are you going to retrieve it later?" I asked, curious about why he'd want to do any such thing.

"I can always get someone at the station to give me a ride. Right now I could use the company."

"That sounds great to me. Hop in," I said, and then George and I followed Jake and Max back into town. "That was all a little too exciting for my taste," I said.

"Really? I haven't felt this alive in years," the mayor and former cop said.

"You miss it, don't you?"

"What's that?"

"Being in danger," I replied.

"That's not it at all, Suzanne."

"Funny, but that's how it seems to me," I said.

After a few minutes of riding in silence, George surprised me by saying, "Maybe you're right after all. There's something invigorating about being in the middle of something like this. I don't have to tell you that though, do I? It's in your blood now too, isn't it?"

I took a moment myself before I answered him. "Honestly, I don't particularly like finding dead bodies or searching for killers, if that's what you're saying."

"Then why do you do it?"

I didn't even have to think about that before I answered. "There's enough injustice in this world in general as it is. If there's something, *anything* I can do to make sure people who commit atrocities like murder are held accountable for their actions, how can I *not* do it? I've thought about stopping my investigations a time or two over the years, but I just can't bring myself to do it."

"We have more in common than you might think," George said. I didn't even have to glance over at him to know that he was smiling.

"I'm okay with the two of us sharing a few traits if you are," I said.

He laughed fully at that comment. "I consider it an honor."

"So do I," I answered. As I pulled into the police station's parking lot beside Max's beat-up old car, I said, "Let's go have a chat with the police chief."

CHAPTER 15

T O NO ONE'S SURPRISE, STEPHEN Grant was still at his desk, despite the late hour. The chief waved us all into his office, a cramped space that had once belonged to Jake. There was barely enough room for all of us, but we stood there as he finished up a telephone call.

"That's right. You can cancel it. He just walked in my door. I know. Sometimes you get lucky. Talk to you later."

"Which one of them were you looking for?" I asked the police chief, though I had a suspicion it was my ex-husband.

"It's Max," he said as he pointed at my ex-husband.

"Listen, I didn't kill Dusty Baxter, and neither did Emily," Max began to protest.

"Did I say that either one of you did?" the chief asked him.

"No," Max admitted reluctantly. "I just figured that I'd get that out of the way up front." He paused for a moment, clearly puzzled. "Let me ask you something. If you don't think I did it, why were you looking for me?"

"I didn't say that I didn't think you did it, either," the chief said. He then turned to Jake and George. "Thanks for bringing him in."

"Hey, I'm standing right here," I told him.

"I saw you," the chief said with the hint of a grin.

I had to laugh, even though I'd just been insulted, at least a little. "Fine. I'm sorry I didn't tell you everything I knew the moment I knew it. Am I forgiven?"

Chief Grant nodded. "Absolutely. Anyway, as much as I appreciate you all coming in, it's a little cramped in here. Mind if Max and I have ourselves a chat?"

"I'm not so sure I'm okay with it," Max said.

The chief leaned back in his chair and studied my ex-husband for a moment. "That's fine with me. We'll do it your way."

"Seriously?" Max asked incredulously. "That's all it's going to take?"

"What do you think?" the chief asked sarcastically. "If you've got legal representation, I'd suggest you give them a call right now. I need to get some information from you, but if you're going to make it difficult on me, then I'm going to return the favor."

Max looked at me. "Is he bluffing?"

I didn't even have to consider the possibility. "No."

"Fine. I'll talk to you, but they stay," my ex said defiantly.

The chief shook his head. "Max, old buddy, that's not the way this works. You don't get to dictate anything right now except your statement."

"Can *Suzanne* at least stay?" he asked plaintively.

"I'm not sure how I feel about that," Jake said.

The chief shrugged. "Let me ask you a question. Can you sit there and stay quiet, Suzanne? I swear the second you say your first word, I'm going to throw you out, in the nicest way possible, of course."

"It's a deal," I said before he could change his mind.

"Suzanne—" Jake started to say before I cut him off.

"Why don't you and George go over to the Boxcar and have some pie? I won't be long."

"I'm not sure I'd promise him that," the chief said. "Max and I have a great deal to discuss."

Jake nodded after he saw my pleading glance. "Fine. George, are you up for a late snack?"

"Do you even have to ask?" the mayor asked him with a grin as he patted his belly soundly.

After they were gone, I took the chair farthest from the chief's desk, while Max sat in the one that was front and center.

"Let's get started," the chief said, ignoring my presence completely. "When is the last time you saw Dusty Baxter alive?"

"Last night," Max said.

Chief Grant nodded, as though he already had that information. "Under what circumstances did you see him?"

Max glanced at me, but before I could give him the go-ahead to tell the chief everything, the police chief added, "I'm asking the questions here. Look at me."

Max did as he was told, and after a few seconds, in a cowed voice, he admitted, "I saw him at Two Cows and a Moose when I unexpectedly got back into town. I'd been in LA filming a commercial, but I came home early to surprise Emily."

"And Dusty was there with her?"

"Yes," Max said.

There was something about the way he said that one word that caught the chief's attention. Max was great when he was delivering lines that someone else had written for him, but when it came to improvising on his own, he was a lot less adept.

"What were they doing?" the chief asked him, staring intently at my ex-husband.

"It looked like he was whispering something in her ear," Max choked out the words.

"You said that's what it *looked* like," the chief said. "What was really happening?"

Max had a choice at that moment. He could tell the police the truth and possibly play a part in hurting his fiancée, or he could lie and set himself up for all kinds of trouble. I was afraid I knew exactly which option he was going to choose.

"Tell him the truth, Max," I urged him.

"That's it, Suzanne. It's time for you to go," the chief said as he stood.

"I was trying to help you!" I couldn't believe that I was getting thrown out for that.

"You knew the rules when we started," he said. "You need to leave, and I mean right now."

"It's okay," Max told me. "I'm going to tell him everything. That's what Emily would want me to do."

It still amazed me how much influence she had over him, when I had managed to garner so little over all of the time that we'd been together.

"Fine. I'm going," I said. Ignoring the chief, I said, "When you finish up, come by the cottage and touch base with us."

"Suzanne, you are already way past your bedtime as it is," Max said.

"I don't care," I said, and then I walked out without even a second glance back at the police chief.

"Wow, that took longer than I thought it would," Jake said as he slid a piece of apple crisp pie in front of me. He and George were halfway finished with theirs.

"Should I resent the fact that you already ordered this for me?" I asked.

"You don't have to eat it," Jake said as he started to reach for the plate.

"I wouldn't do that if I were you," I said as I handled my fork like a weapon.

"What happened?" George asked. "What did you say that got you thrown out?"

"I was trying to urge Max to tell the truth, and I got tossed out for it. Can you believe that?" Jake was suspiciously silent, so I asked him, "You don't think he was right to do it, do you?" All my husband would do was shrug, which was enough of a reply for me. "Suddenly I don't much feel like having pie."

"I'll eat it if you don't want it," George said as he reached for it.

"Okay. You called my bluff," I said as I grabbed it tightly.

"You know I'm right, don't you?" Jake asked me softly.

"Why do you think I'm angry about it? Of course you're right. I just thought he'd make an exception if I was trying to help him."

"Do you think Max will really incriminate Emily?" George asked.

"He was about to do just that when I left," I replied.

"Why would he do something like that?" George asked.

"If I were in his shoes, I would have done the exact same thing," Jake said, surprising George but not me.

"You're kidding. Why?" George asked, honestly curious about my husband's answer.

"Because that's exactly what Emily would have expected him to do, and I knew if we were in the same position, Suzanne would accept nothing less herself."

I patted his hand and smiled at him. "You're forgiven."

"I didn't realize I needed it, but I'll take it anyway. Thanks."

"You're welcome," I said as I took my first bite of pie. Just as I did, I heard my mother's voice behind my chair.

"Suzanne, are you sure you should be eating this late? Why aren't you in bed? Don't you have a donut shop to run in the morning?"

I looked at my mother and smiled. "Gee, Mom, Jake asked me out on a date, so how could I say no? I know it's a school night, but all of my homework's done, and besides, he's so cute I couldn't bring myself to say no. Please don't ground me."

Momma stared hard at me for a full two seconds, and then she laughed loudly enough to garner the attention of the other patrons at the Boxcar Grill. "Your humor is extremely odd. You know that, don't you?"

"Know it? I relish it," I said. "Why don't you and Phillip pull up two chairs and join us? We'll be glad to scooch over and make room for you."

"Dot, you can have my spot. I was just about to leave anyway," George said.

"Nonsense, Mr. Mayor. I wouldn't dream of it."

George grinned at her. "Well, I outrank you, though I wouldn't if you'd taken the job instead of me. Good night, folks." He added as an aside to Jake, "Let me know if anything comes up."

"Will do," Jake said.

"How are you going to get your truck?" I asked him.

"I won't have any trouble getting another ride," he said, and I knew that it was true. Since he'd become our mayor, George had become a popular figure around town. I thought it was because he was a politician who actually meant what he said and acted accordingly.

As Momma and Phillip joined us, Trish came by and made the dirty dishes vanish. "What can I get for you folks tonight?"

"Everyone else has pie, so I'd like some myself," Phillip said.

"Don't you get enough of that at home?" Momma asked me.

Her husband looked shocked by the suggestion. "Enough pie? Is there even such a thing? Jake, back me up here."

I knew that my husband didn't want to cross my mother even in fun, but he took a deep breath, grinned, and then said, "That's always been my attitude."

Momma shook her head, but I could see her trying her best to hide her smile. "Men."

"Does that mean that *you* don't want pie, Mrs. Hart?"

She raised an eyebrow in Trish's direction. "Whatever gave you that impression? We'll have two slices, please."

"Any particular kind?" Trish asked her with a grin.

"Surprise us," Momma said, answering it.

"Consider it done," Trish said.

Momma looked at her husband. "Are you okay with me ordering for the both of us?"

"Are you kidding? I'm getting pie! There's no way I'm going to be disappointed, no matter what kind she brings me." Phillip turned to look at me as he added, "That must have been tough finding Dusty's body like that."

"Jake was there, too," I said. I didn't even have to ask how he knew. Word, especially when it involved murder, spread through our little town faster than a brush fire in August.

"Sure, but he's used to it, I'm sure." Addressing Jake directly, he added, "As much as you can get used to that kind of thing, that is."

"I take your point," Jake said.

"So, who do you think did it?" Momma asked me.

"I don't know," I replied. It was true enough. I had my suspicions and more than a couple of suspects, but I didn't know anything definitively at that point.

"But you're investigating, right?" Momma asked.

"What makes you ask that?"

"Suzanne, are you honestly going to keep up this charade?"

"No," I said, suddenly too tired to banter with her. "Jake and I are looking into it."

I was expecting a scolding, but instead, Momma simply nodded. "Good. I'm glad."

"Hang on a second," I said. "Since when are you happy that I'm digging into murder?"

"You and Jake found the poor man. Of course you've got a reason to investigate the crime. Just promise me one thing."

"I'll be careful," I said.

"Good, but that's not what I wanted you to promise," Momma answered.

"Sorry. I didn't mean to jump the gun. What do you want me to promise you?"

"That no matter who killed that unfortunate man, you'll do your best to see them punished for the crime," Momma said.

It was an odd thing for her to say. "What are you getting at, Momma?"

"I know how close you are to Emily, and for reasons that defy all explanation, that ex-husband of yours as well, but if the signs point to either one of them as being guilty, you can't let that sway your judgment or your actions."

"I'm willing to admit that it would be hard on me, but I wouldn't handle things any other way," I answered. "And just in case I was ever tempted, which I wouldn't be, I've got Jake. He'll make sure I do the right thing if I start to waver."

"You won't need me," my husband said as he patted my hand. "You almost always do the right thing, Suzanne."

"Almost?" I asked him with a grin.

"Man, that's good pie. I may have another piece," Jake said as Trish brought slices of cherry crumble pie to Momma and Phillip, completely ignoring my question. That was fine by me.

"I think we've had enough," I said as I stood. "As everyone keeps pointing out, I have an early day tomorrow, so I'm afraid I have to say good night." I leaned over and kissed my mother's cheek. "I love you, Momma."

"I love you, too, Suzanne. Sleep well."

"I'll do my best," I said.

After Jake paid our bill, we walked to my Jeep together in the glow from a streetlight. "It would be simpler to walk home than to drive back," I said.

"Sure, but then you won't have me to escort you back through the park in the middle of the night when you go to work in a few hours," he replied.

"It's April Springs, for goodness sake," I said. "What could happen?"

"You really don't expect me to answer that, do you?" Jake asked me.

"No, I suppose not. With a murderer on the loose, nobody can be too careful."

"Agreed," Jake replied. I drove the short distance around the block to our cottage, slowing down at Grace's place. I could see she was home, and the flashing images from the television told me that she was watching something. I'd have to let her know what I was up to, but then again, I was pretty sure her boyfriend, Chief Grant, would do that for me.

As I parked in my spot beside Jake's truck, I glanced over at our front porch.

Someone was sitting there in the dark, waiting for us.

Was it a benign visit, or was the killer paying us a call?

CHAPTER 16

"**J**AKE, DO YOU SEE THAT? Someone's on our porch. Do you think it's Max?"

"I don't see how it could be. There's no way the chief is finished with him yet," my husband said as he drew out his weapon. I'd nearly forgotten that he'd been carrying it, even after we'd been shot at not two hours earlier. That was the way my mind worked sometimes, compartmentalizing things to the point where one day seemed like several all strung together in a row. After all, we'd just found Dusty's body that afternoon, as hard as that was for me to believe.

A great deal had happened since then, almost none of it good.

"Max? Is that you?" I called out before Jake could approach the porch.

"No. It's Emily," she said as she stepped out of the shadows. "Why did you ask me that? Is Max coming?"

"As soon as he's finished at the police station," I said. "Come on in."

"I know it's late for you. I shouldn't have come," Emily said as she stepped off the porch and started toward the park.

"Nonsense," I said as I turned the light on. "I'll be up for a while yet. Come on in. I was just about to make some hot chocolate. I could brew up some coffee for you, if you prefer."

I'd had no intention of doing either, but if my friend was there, I was guessing she had a good reason, and I wasn't about to turn her away just to get a little sleep.

"If you're sure," she said a little reluctantly.

"Of course we're sure," Jake said.

"Thanks. I appreciate that," Emily said as she followed us inside the cottage.

"Let's go into the kitchen so we can all chat," I suggested as we took our jackets off. The days were definitely getting warmer, but the nights could still have a bite to them.

As Jake and Emily took up chairs at the kitchen table, I got busy making hot chocolate. I had a mix I loved, and Jake had instantly become a fan, too. We sold it at Donut Hearts when Emma wasn't being wildly experimental with our beverage offerings, which was a great deal of the time lately. For the most part, I handled the donuts while she came up with new drink combinations. The range and scope of coffee flavors she found truly amazed me, but in the cold months, she'd started playing around with our hot chocolate recipes, too.

I could have microwaved the milk and started serving drinks in less than two minutes, but this occasion seemed to call for using a teakettle on the range to heat the liquid. While it was warming up, it would give us a chance to chat.

"It will just be a few minutes," I said as I got three carrot-cake cupcakes out of the fridge and plated them. They were Jake's favorites, so I'd made him a batch the day before. In all honesty, it kind of surprised me that there were still three left. "Would anyone like a cupcake?"

"I'll take one," Jake volunteered, even though he'd just polished off a large slab of pie at the Boxcar Grill.

"I'd love one, too. I'm starving, actually," Emily said as she took one.

"I can make you a proper meal in no time at all if you're

hungry," I said. For a moment, I sounded just like my mother, something that caused me to frown but would have probably amused her to no end.

"Thanks anyway, but this is perfect," she said as she took a bite. "Wow, that's delicious. Did you make it from scratch?"

"No, it's just a mix," I admitted.

"One that she embellishes in her own way," Jake said proudly.

I didn't have the heart to tell him that I just added a pinch of cinnamon, a dash of nutmeg, and the slightest whisper of vanilla paste. If he chose to think that made me a master baker, then who was I to dissuade him? "What's going on, Emily? How are the guys? What's going on with them?"

"The truth is, I have a feeling that they're more than a bit traumatized by what's happened," she said.

"Does the police chief still have custody of them?" I asked.

To Jake's credit, he didn't look at either one of us as though we were crazy, which in retrospect he had every right to do.

"No, I got them back fifteen minutes ago after Chief Grant questioned me at the station. I couldn't bear to leave them alone at the newsstand, so I took them home and tucked them into my bed before I came over here to speak with you."

"How did your interview with the police go?" I asked tentatively.

"As you suggested, I told Chief Grant everything, including Dusty's behavior last night," Emily admitted. "It wasn't easy to do, but what choice did I have? I had to tell the truth."

"Did you ever find out who came into the newsstand last night?" Jake asked her.

I shot him a reproachful look, but it was too late to do anything about it now.

"No, but that wasn't even a factor in my decision. I learned a long time ago that the truth was always the best option, no matter how bad a light it might shine on me," Emily said. "Why? Do you know who it was?"

I looked at Jake, wondering if I should tell her, but he merely shrugged. No doubt he wanted to avoid another nonverbal scolding from me if he could. Maybe if I told her now, it would give her time to accept it when she finally saw her fiancé. "It was Max," I said, watching her carefully.

I'd expected her to be angry for a number of reasons, but she merely looked confused. "Max? That's not possible. He's back in town? What about his commercial?"

"Evidently it fell through, so he came back early," I said, not wanting to muddy the water with news of his abrupt termination. "He said he wanted to surprise you."

"Then why didn't he come in when he saw me with Dusty?"

Jake answered softly, "He wasn't sure what he was interrupting."

Instead of being angry that Max hadn't come to her rescue, Emily was suddenly stricken by another thought. "Oh, no. I can't imagine what it must have looked like to him. The poor dear must have thought I was carrying on with Dusty. He must have been heartbroken! No wonder he ran away." She looked genuinely distraught by the thought as she suddenly stood. "I've got to find him this instant and explain it to him."

"Emily, he's on his way over here as soon as he can get free," I said, knowing that it was what he'd promised to do but being unsure of the exact timeline. That was up to the police chief, but I believed that it was true nonetheless. I stood and felt the steam coming off the hot milk. After I turned the burner off, I poured equal portions of milk into mugs, already waiting with the delicious powdery mix. After stirring each mug in turn, I distributed them as I urged Emily to sit back down.

She finally agreed, and after taking a sip, she said, "I'm not sure I can just sit around and wait for Max to show up."

"It's not exactly something you can rush. He's being interviewed by the police chief right now," Jake said. "You might as well wait for him here."

"Emily, at this very moment he's telling the chief what he saw last night, or at least what he thought he saw," I said.

"Of course he is," Emily said proudly. "It's what I would urge him to do if he'd come to me first. There can't be *any* secrets between us, and I won't have him, or anyone else for that matter, lying for me, most especially to the police. I know that now."

"How did *you* leave things with the chief?" Jake asked her gently.

"I'm not supposed to leave town, not that I had any big trips planned or anything," she said. "I had the distinct impression that I'm at the top of his list of suspects." She didn't even seem that upset by the prospect.

"And that doesn't bother you?" I asked her after taking a sip of cocoa myself. It was, as always, amazing, but at the moment, the nuanced flavors were lost on me.

"Of course it does," she said in a level voice, "but who can blame him? If I didn't know better, I would think the same thing myself."

Jake suddenly asked, "Emily, you said you were with the police chief earlier. How long have you been here waiting for us?"

"I left his office, dropped the guys off at home, and then I came straight here," she said.

"Did you speak with anyone from the time you left home to the time you came here?"

"As a matter of fact, I talked to Grace for at least five minutes before I got to your place. She wanted to know how I was doing. She's really sweet, isn't she? Why do you want to know where I was?"

"Relax, it's good news. Given the timeline, it means that you can prove that you didn't shoot at Max, which in turn tells me that you didn't kill Dusty, either," Jake said.

Emily looked thoroughly confused now. "Someone shot Max? Is he hurt? Why didn't you tell me that before?" Emily stood up, spilling her hot chocolate as she ran for the door.

I was about to try to stop her when someone else did, as she ran straight into Max's arms.

"Are you okay?" she asked him as she searched for any sign of a wound. "I thought you'd been shot."

"Shot at," I corrected her, but she wasn't paying any attention to me at all.

"Emily, I'm fine," he said as he hugged her. "I had to tell the police about you and Dusty. I'm so sorry," he said, his voice coming out in almost a sob.

"You did the right thing," she said, stroking his hair lightly. "Don't worry. Everything is going to be fine."

Max pulled back a little and stared into her eyes. I felt a little like a voyeur, but hey, they were standing in my kitchen, so I couldn't exactly excuse myself. Well, I could have, but I wasn't going to. As I cleaned up the spilled hot chocolate, I heard Max ask, "How about you? Are you okay?"

"I'm just dandy, now that you're back," she said, hugging him fiercely again.

"I'm sorry I didn't trust you," Max said, choking out the words.

"What choice did you have?" she asked. "I understand."

"At least you should both be in the clear now," I said.

"I'm just hoping we can convince the police of that," Jake said.

"What do you mean?" I asked him.

"We believe that because she didn't shoot at Max, she didn't kill Dusty," Jake said, "but there's no guarantee that the police chief will see it the same way. The shot at Max might not have anything to do with Dusty's murder."

"She didn't do it," Max said as he took a step toward Jake. I admired his spunk, but my husband would have killed him if it came down to a physical confrontation between the two of them.

Fortunately for all concerned, Emily stepped between them. "Let's all take a deep breath, shall we? Max, let's get out of here. Suzanne needs to get at least a little sleep before she opens the shop tomorrow, and you and I need to spend some time together."

"I couldn't agree more," Max said eagerly.

"Talking," Emily added.

"Oh. Okay. Of course. You're right." He seemed genuinely disappointed there wouldn't be more to their interaction, and it was all I could do not to laugh out loud. Some things about the man never changed.

After they were gone, Jake put the mugs in the sink and rinsed them.

"Do you honestly think Chief Grant is going to think the shooting at the cabin isn't in some way related to Dusty's murder?" I asked him.

"No, probably not. I'm likely just jumping at shadows. It's been quite a day. Will you be able to get at least a little sleep before you have to go in to work tomorrow?"

"You're kidding, right? I'll be asleep before my head hits the pillow."

"I don't know how you do it," Jake said.

"It's easy, really. Exhaustion is the perfect sleeping pill. Are you coming to bed?"

"I'll be in a little later. There are a few things I want to ponder tonight."

"Fine," I said as I kissed him good night. "Just promise me you won't go off and do something on your own."

"I promise, at least for tonight," he said with a grin.

"That's all that I can ask for," I replied, smiling in return.

I was wrong, though. Sleep didn't come easily at all. I must have tossed and turned for half an hour before I finally drifted off.

I had a hunch that tomorrow was going to be a very long day indeed.

And I didn't even know the half of it yet.

CHAPTER 17

"WHAT HAPPENED? DID I GET our schedules mixed up?" I asked Emma as I walked into the donut shop bright and early the next morning and found her sitting on a stool. "I could swear this was your day off."

"I'm not here to work. We need to talk, Suzanne," Emma said.

Oh, no. I'd lost Emma once for a short period of time when she'd gone off to college and then again when she'd helped her boyfriend open his new restaurant. Was this going to be her third and final exit from my business and my daily life? "You're leaving, aren't you?" I asked, slumping back against the wall. So much for my plan to take the news gracefully.

"Leaving? Why would I do that? I just got here."

"I mean the shop," I said as I pulled off my jacket.

"Suzanne, I'm not going anywhere until you throw me out," Emma said. "You're not throwing me out, are you?"

"No, that's never going to happen." I felt immensely better. "So, if you're not here tendering your resignation, why are you here so early? Insomnia?"

"As a matter of fact, I haven't even been to bed yet," she said. "I just left Emily's house."

"Funny, she was with Max when she left my place," I said as I flipped on the fryer. As I started doing my daily chores by mostly muscle memory, I asked, "What happened? Did they have a fight?"

"No. It's quite the opposite, in fact. I think they're going to elope," Emma said, the concern obvious in her voice.

"Well, I can't blame them. They tried to have a formal wedding once and someone ended up dying," I said, remembering the obnoxious best man who hadn't made it to the final day.

"I don't, either," Emma said, and then she bit her lower lip for a moment. "I just don't want her rushing into anything."

"I thought you liked Max," I said as I started measuring out the ingredients for the cake donuts. I always started the day with cake donuts, and then I moved on to the raised ones. It was a system that I'd perfected over the years, and I wasn't about to change it, though I knew that Emma did things her own way when she was in charge of the shop two days a week.

"I do. At least I did," Emma said. "Dad told me something last night that kind of rattled me, though."

I couldn't imagine what Ray Blake might tell her, but if I knew the newspaperman, it wasn't anything good. "Don't believe everything you hear," I said. I wanted to add, "especially from your father," but I didn't have the heart to do it.

"Dad said he heard that Max implicated Emily in Dusty's murder last night."

I couldn't argue the point, but sometimes perspective was everything. "Did he say how he did that, exactly?" I asked as I continued to measure and add ingredients.

"Dad got a tip from someone at the police station that Max told them that he'd seen Emily and Dusty together in the newsstand through the window the night before last, and what was worse, they were in a compromising position."

So far, it appeared that old Ray had gotten the straight scoop, though his interpretation of the events was likely to be suspect. "What did Emily say? I'm sure you asked her about it."

"You'd better believe I did!"

"So? What was her answer?"

"She said that she loved Max, and only Max! What hold does that man have over normally nice and sweet and sane girls, Suzanne?"

"Jake asked me the same thing. You know, I might not be the right person to ask that question of," I said.

"I'd say you're *exactly* the right one," Emma replied. "No offense or disrespect intended, but you fell for Max first."

"Trust me, there was a long line of women before me, and after as well, I'm sure," I said.

"You know what I mean," Emma persisted. "I'm honestly worried about her marrying him."

"Did you tell her that, in those exact words?" I asked as I finished adding the basic ingredients to my cake donut mix. It was only after I had a solid base to work with that I began dividing up portions into separate bowls and tweaking each individual flavor I offered for sale.

"I did. She told me that he confessed it all to her, and that she not only forgave him, but she approved of him telling Chief Grant! Is that the act of a sane woman, I ask you?"

I stopped what I was doing and patted Emma's hand. "It sounds as though she's in love with him and that she trusts him to do the right thing."

"Suzanne, in my wildest imagination, I never dreamed you'd approve of this," Emma said with a pouting lower lip.

"What can I say? Max has changed," I said for the thousandth time that year. It was difficult sometimes defending my ex-husband's character, especially after how our marriage had ended, but in my mind, and clearly in Emily's as well, he'd done the right thing, even if I had been forced to coax him a bit to get him to do it.

"I guess so," Emma said as she stood and reached for her

jacket. "Anyway, I just wanted to talk to you about it. You've certainly given me something to think about."

"Sorry I couldn't be more sympathetic to your point of view," I said. "If you'd like, you could always hang around and help me make donuts. That's bound to give you time to think." I'd been joking, plain and simple, just trying to coax a smile from her.

To my surprise, Emma hung her coat back up and reached for her apron. "Do you know what? I think I will."

"Emma, I was just teasing."

"I know that, but I've got a lot to process right now, so I know I'll never get to sleep. Making donuts will help me distance myself a bit from what's going on."

"Will doing dishes serve the same purpose?" I asked her with a grin. When I was away, Emma made the donuts and her mother, Sharon, took over her chores, but when I was in charge, Emma was the one who kept everything clean and neat.

"Sure. Why not? You don't even have to pay me!"

"You know, a lot of folks have used washing dishes as therapy," I said with a grin.

"Really?"

"How should I know?" I asked with a laugh as I tossed a nearby hand towel in her direction. "But there's only one way to find out if it works." I had no intention of letting her work for free, though. In fact, if I could afford it, I was going to pay her time and a half. After all, it was her day off.

"I'll let you know," she said as she got busy setting up the front for me. Even when Emma came in on her regularly scheduled days, she wasn't there that early. I liked to time her arrival at somewhere close to the moment that I started dropping the first cake donuts into the hot oil. While they cooked, Emma handled things out front, and once I was finished swinging the dangerous dough dropper, forcing the dough to the bottom where I could get it to drop into the oil—hence its name—she was ready to step in and make things clean again.

Once the cake donut selection for the day was finished, iced, and on the cooling racks, I went out front to get Emily so she could start on the dishes.

I found her fast asleep, curled up on one of our couches.

Smiling, I grabbed my jacket and made an impromptu blanket from it, covering her, at least mostly.

She didn't even stir.

The poor thing was clearly exhausted.

I took in the scene of her resting, and then I headed back into the kitchen to start the first round of dishes myself.

As I washed and dried the items I'd used so far, I thought about where things stood with our list of suspects. I was delighted to eliminate Max and Emily from my list, no matter what anyone else might think. After all, it stood to reason that if Max had killed Dusty, then who took the shot at him at the lake? It couldn't have been Emily. She had the best alibi of all, being interviewed by the police chief right around the time the attack on Max had occurred. I supposed that it was possible that the shot wasn't related to Dusty's murder, but I simply found that impossible to believe. There was no way that particular coincidence made any sense at all. No, I needed to work off the assumption that whoever had stabbed Dusty had taken that shot at Max. But why? I had a difficult time imagining either of my final two suspects shooting at Max in the darkness. Could Michelle be more familiar with firearms than she appeared to be? I wouldn't have thought she'd be able to identify most weapons, let alone fire them. Hattie could have learned how to shoot for a play, but the question kept rearing its ugly head: why shoot at Max at all? Was it possible that my ex-husband knew more about this case than he realized? Did someone feel threatened enough by his knowledge to try to stop him from talking before he figured it out? If that was the case, I needed to speak to him again before the killer could strike.

Despite the early hour, I dried my hands and grabbed my cell phone.

It wasn't a great surprise when my call went straight to voicemail.

"Max, this is Suzanne. Call me as soon as you get this, and I mean immediately. It could be important."

That done, I finished up the dishes. It had surprised me by how quickly the stack had been finished, and it was undeniable that I felt better.

Maybe there was something to this dishwashing therapy after all.

As I hung up the towel to dry, the kitchen door opened. Emma came in, rubbing the sleep from her eyes. "I fell asleep."

"Did you?" I asked her with a grin.

"You know I did. I believe this is yours," she said as she handed me my jacket. "Why didn't you wake me?"

"You looked so comfortable, I couldn't bring myself to do it," I admitted. "Why don't you go on and head home? I've got this covered, and you could clearly use some sleep."

"Are you sure?" Emma asked, clearly hoping that I wasn't going to change my mind.

"I'm positive," I said. "Now off with you, young lady."

"Thanks, Suzanne. For everything," she added as she hugged me for a brief few seconds. It was a rare treat from my employee, and more importantly, my friend.

"You're most welcome. It's going to be all right. Trust me."

"I always do," she said, and then she headed home.

Once again I had the donut shop to myself.

After a bit more work, I had the yeast donut dough ready to go through its first rest/proof. That was normally the time Emma and I took our break outside, no matter what the time of year or the weather. I thought about staying in this one time, but after setting the timer, I found myself reaching for my jacket and heading outside despite my best intentions.

Once I was outside sitting on one of the few chairs we kept for our al fresco diners, I began to get the eerie feeling that someone was watching me. Every time I thought I saw someone in the shadows, I ultimately decided that it was more likely my overactive imagination than someone actually being there.

Or so I thought at the time.

CHAPTER 18

I WAS SORELY TEMPTED WITH THE idea of going back inside
Donut Hearts despite the fact that I had seven minutes left
on the timer in my hand. I normally wasn't so jumpy, but
after all, Dusty had just been murdered, and someone had taken
a shot at Max. Presumably Max had been the intended victim.
Was it possible that someone had been going after Jake, the
mayor, or even me? No, I felt as though I could safely rule myself
out. While Jake, Max, and George could pass for each other, at
least as shadows in the dark, nobody was about to mistake my
silhouette for any of theirs. Hey, maybe it was finally paying off
that I was so curvy.

At least it kept me out of the shooting gallery.

"Suzanne?" I heard someone call out to me as I turned to go
back inside. It was a woman, but that was all that I could tell
from the voice.

It clearly hadn't been my imagination after all.

"Who's there? Step out of the shadows so I can see you."

"Is anyone with you?" she asked timidly, and finally, I could
tell that it was Hattie Moon.

"No. Hattie, stop hiding in the dark."

"Emma's still there, isn't she?" the older actress asked me as
she took one step forward.

"No, she left after she fell asleep on the couch. How long have
you been standing out here waiting for me to come outside?"

"I showed up right after you did," she admitted. "I was about to knock on the door when I spotted Emma inside with you through the kitchen door. Are you *sure* she's gone?"

"Hattie, even if she *were* here, which she's not, you wouldn't have anything to fear from her, either. Now come on in. I've got fresh cake donuts and coffee inside, and you are welcome to some of each."

"I like yeast ones best," Hattie said as she joined me. Once she was in the light, I could see that she was quite a bit worse for the wear. She had a few scratches on her face and her hands, and her muumuu was smudged in a few places.

"So do I, but cake donuts are delightful, too. Besides, the yeast donuts aren't ready yet." I gestured to her state of disorder. "What happened, did you say the wrong thing to a cat?"

"I got caught in some bushes over there while I was waiting for you," she said as she pointed to the park across the street. I supposed that it might be possible to get scratched up like that from them, but I had a more likely, and more condemning, idea as to how she had collected those scratches, and when.

"Were you out at the lake last night, by any chance?" I asked her as she walked into the light of Donut Hearts behind me. There was that ever-present powerful aroma of perfume on her, something that she always overused, at least in my opinion. I wasn't sure where she bought her scent, but I had a hunch it was sold in industrial-sized vats by the way she went through it. I'd noticed it before at her house and then again outside the shop, but up close and in a confined space, it was nearly overpowering.

"No. I haven't been out there for ages. Why do you ask?"

"No reason," I said, which was a complete and utter lie. Whoever had taken that shot at Max had been forced to circle around on the path in order to get a clear shot at him, and if they were stumbling around in the dark, it could certainly be reasonable to assume that they got a little scratched up and maybe even smudged in the process. I poured us both some coffee and grabbed a pair of apple cinnamon cake donuts, one for each of us. I was experimenting with not only using apple cinnamon pie filling inside but also using bits of cut-up apple dusted with cinnamon in the batter itself. I still wasn't one hundred percent satisfied with the results, but I was getting close.

Hattie took a bite and then smiled. "Wow, that's really good."

"Thanks. It's still a work in progress at this point."

"If you ask me, I'd say that your work is finished," she said. "May I possibly have another?"

So much for her not liking cake donuts. I grabbed another one for her, and she ate it quickly as well. "Hattie, have you had dinner?"

"No, I had to skip it last night," she reported with a frown.

"Why on earth would you have to do that?"

"I couldn't go home last night. Someone's been watching my house," she said gravely.

"You're not talking about Jake and me, are you?" I asked her as I grabbed her a third donut. Ordinarily I wouldn't have recommended three donuts in one sitting for the tiny woman, but these were extenuating circumstances. Besides, chances were good that if I kept feeding her, she'd hang around for my questions.

"What? No, of course not."

"Then who was it?"

"I have no idea," she said brusquely.

Suddenly I got it. "You didn't see anyone yourself, but I'm willing to bet that Millie Farnsworth did." Since Millie, Hattie's personal neighborhood watch, had reported our visit to her, it only followed that she'd report any *other* trespassers or unwelcome visitors to Hattie's place.

"Millie is just looking out for me," Hattie said in her neighbor's defense.

"Did she happen to say who it was?" I asked her.

"No, she couldn't tell, but she is positive that someone was there. She called me on my cell phone and warned me to stay away, and I've been afraid to go back home ever since."

"You need to call the police," I said as I poured her a little more coffee. I'd taken a bite of the cake donut as well, and I thought Hattie just might be right. This one might finally be ready for prime time in the form of a spot on the menu.

"The chief is the last person I care to see right now," she said. "He is under the impression that I killed Dusty Baxter."

"Did he come right out and say that to you?" I asked her, startled to think that the chief would make such an accusation without having solid proof.

"No, but he didn't have to. You may not know this about me, but I'm a master at reading nuance and innuendo."

Somehow I kind of doubted that. "Hattie, I can tell you right now that he's not that sure."

"How can you possibly know that? Has he said something to you?" The older actress leaned forward, eager to hear my answer.

"He didn't have to. If he thought you did it, you'd be locked up right now." I was pretty sure that my reasoning there was on solid ground.

"Nonsense," she said, but clearly she was a little relieved by my explanation.

"The way I see it, you have two choices, Hattie. You can call the police and get them to investigate your prowler, or you can keep hiding until the real killer is found, which might be a very long time from now."

She frowned at me, took the last bite of her third donut, washed it down with coffee, and then she headed for the door.

Hattie's hand was on the handle when I said, "Oh, there's

just one more thing. If you don't call them, I'm going to do it myself."

"Suzanne Hart, this is none of your business," she said with a little too much indignation for my taste. Then again, Hattie always did tend to overact.

"Maybe so, but your presence here this morning has made it mine. The choice is up to you. You call them, or I will."

After pausing for a few moments, she finally sighed. "Fine. I'll make the call."

Hattie was starting out again when I said, "I meant that you should do it right now, in front of me."

"Are you saying that you don't trust me?" she asked me a little too incredulously for my taste.

"Of course I do," I said with a grin that was as false as one of her scenes on stage. As my smile faded, I took out my own cell phone and pretended to prepare to make a call.

That was all it took.

She had her phone out and was dialing before I had to do anything else. "Yes, I'd like to report a prowler. No, I won't stay inside the house. I'm not there. Yes. You are correct. This is Hattie Moon. Have your officer come to the donut shop when he's finished. I'll be waiting there for him. Yes. Of course. Good-bye."

After she hung up, Hattie asked me, "Are you satisfied?"

"You bet."

I hadn't planned on her camping out until the police checked for the presence of a prowler, but I could hardly complain, given the fact that I'd forced her to call myself. "While you're waiting, I'll pour you another cup of coffee."

My timer went off just then. It was time to tend to the dough for the yeast donuts. "I'll be in the kitchen if you need me," I said as I walked back.

Hattie was close on my heels. "Where do you think you're going? I can't stay out here all alone. What if I'm in danger?"

"You're welcome to come back into the kitchen with me, but I have work to do if folks are going to get their raised donuts this morning."

Hattie reluctantly followed me back, and as I worked, she kept watching me with a critical eye. It was worse than if she'd provided negative commentary throughout the process, and in the even tighter quarters, her scent was overpowering. I'd have to trust my instincts on the donuts I made. My sense of smell, and therefore taste, was going to be shot for a while.

I was about to say something about Hattie's lurking when she spoke instead. "There's quite a bit of work that goes into making those, isn't there?"

"It's a fair amount, but I don't mind. In fact, I kind of enjoy the process." That was a good thing, too. If I didn't, I'd thrown away a good chunk of my life doing something that I didn't really like. I knew there were a lot of folks who did just that, but I'd rather be poor and happy than rich and miserable. Then again, I'd never been rich, so who was I to say? Still, I was pretty sure that I'd feel the same way, and if I suddenly won the lottery, I'd be hard pressed to give up making donuts forever.

I wouldn't mind the opportunity to find out if that were true or not, though.

"You put so much time and energy into them and sell them for so little. Not only that, but by tomorrow, they'll all be gone, and the process has to start all over again."

"Isn't acting on the stage the same thing?" I asked her. "Your performance is gone as soon as you give it, and the next night, you have to start all over again."

"Suzanne, are you honestly trying to compare my art to you making donuts?" Her indignation was real, and it was all I could do not to laugh.

I was about to try to say something to mollify her when there was a tap at the front door. "That will be the police, unless I miss my guess." I probably should have been grateful for the interruption, since it had saved me from saying something I would probably regret later.

"Probably" was the key word.

It was indeed an April Springs police officer, but it was one I hadn't had much contact with in the past. She was a tall and husky woman, but it didn't appear that she had an ounce of fat on her. I knew one thing. If a fight broke out nearby, I'd want her to have my back.

"Hey, I'm Suzanne. I don't think we've ever formally met," I said as I opened the door. "Would you like some coffee?"

"No, thanks," she said. "I'm Hillary Watts, by the way. I'd take you up on your offer, but the coffee might keep me awake." Her grin was contagious.

"Isn't that a good thing while you're on duty?"

"This is my last call," she said with a smile. "Where exactly did you see the prowler?"

I had been mistaken for many things in the past, but never Hattie Moon. Where was she, anyway? Probably cowering in back. "Hattie. The police would like to speak with you."

The actress came out, albeit a little reluctantly. "Did you catch him?" she asked Officer Watts tentatively.

"No, ma'am. I couldn't see any signs that anyone had been there."

Hattie frowned hard at the officer before she spoke again. "Are you calling Millie Farnsworth a liar?"

"Ma'am, I'm fairly new in town and to this police force, but I've been a cop for seven years. Ms. Farnsworth, I didn't mean to imply that you were a liar."

That upset Hattie more than my art comment had. "Do you honestly think *I* am Millie?"

"I thought you were referring to yourself in the third person," Officer Watts said, trying to hide the beginning of a smile.

I liked her already.

"I wouldn't dream of doing anything so pedestrian," Hattie said.

"Listen, if you'd like, I'd be happy to follow you home and look around again, but I didn't see any signs that anyone had been there."

"Despite what my *neighbor*, Millie Farnsworth, saw?" Hattie asked.

"All I can tell you is that *I* didn't see anything," she said.

"I can see myself home. My tricycle is parked over in the bushes." Hattie shook her head indignantly and stormed out of the donut shop without even a thank you for the food and coffee I'd provided.

"I guess I'll see you later," Officer Watts said. "It was nice to meet you."

"Likewise. Stop by anytime. Chances are that I'll be here," I said.

After all the excitement of having a visitor in the middle of the night died down, it was time to get back to work. After all, I didn't have that much time before I would have to open the shop and start selling my treats. Hattie might not have thought much of it, but it was part of a life I'd worked very hard to have for myself, and I loved every second of it.

Well, *almost* every second.

CHAPTER 19

"**H**EY, MICHELLE. IT'S FUNNY SEEING you here," I said as I opened the donut shop for business at the appointed hour. "You usually don't come by Donut Hearts." In fact, she'd told me before that she thought my pastry treats were poison.

"What can I say? I might not care for what you sell here, but I thought I'd get my bosses a treat before work today," she said as she walked in past me and headed straight for the display case. "What's the best thing you make?"

"Would you believe me if I said that everything was delicious?" I asked her. It was odd seeing her in my shop, though not as odd as it had been seeing Hattie earlier while I'd been making donuts. When people were suspects in my investigations, they often used coming by the shop as an excuse to pry and probe to see what I knew, whether they were guilty of murder or not. I didn't mind. It ultimately served two functions: I had another chance to see them without having to track them down myself, and I sold more treats, which was a win-win in my book.

"Come on. Some of your baked goods must be more popular than others," she answered with a frown. "Why don't you make up a dozen of the ones you sell the most of in the course of a day?"

"I can do that," I said as I started collecting plain glazed, chocolate glazed, old-fashioned cake, lemon-filled, Boston cream, and a few other select choices. It wasn't the most imaginative dozen donuts I'd ever put together, but I had a hunch that they weren't the real reason she was visiting me. I had a couple of choices. *I* could bring up Dusty's murder, or I could let *her*. I decided to see how long it took her to mention it. After I collected her money and handed over the box, I began to wonder just how sound my strategy was turning out to be. As Michelle started for the door, I saw her hesitate. Finally we were getting somewhere.

And then George Morris walked in and spoiled everything.

"Can I get the door for you?" George asked her gallantly as he did just that, holding it wide open for her.

"Sure. That's sweet of you," Michelle said, clearly a little unnerved by the mayor's sudden appearance.

"Before you go, was there something you wanted to talk to me about, Michelle?" I asked her before she walked out.

"No. I just came by for the donuts."

I didn't believe that for one second, but I couldn't exactly detain her until she talked to me.

After she was gone, George frowned at me. "Suzanne, did I just ruin something?"

"I think she was about to tell me something about our murder investigation," I admitted. There was no reason to sugarcoat things with George, and he felt the same way with me. It certainly saved us both a lot of tiptoeing around each other.

"Blast it. I'll see what I can find out," he said, and before I could stop him, he raced out after Michelle.

"George," I called out, hoping to stop him, but either he didn't hear me, or he chose not to listen.

I had a hunch I knew which scenario it was.

As I sold donuts and coffee for the next hour and a half, I couldn't stop wondering what Michelle had really wanted. In fact, I got so distracted by it that I tried to give Gabby Williams change for a twenty instead of the ten she'd given me for her coffee. "I can see why you're constantly on the edge of bankruptcy," Gabby said with her usual charm as she handed me back half of her change.

"Sorry, my mind was somewhere else."

"Clearly," Gabby said with the hint of a frown. I knew she was beaming on the inside, having caught me in a boneheaded mistake. We were friends, at least by the oddest of definitions, and I knew that my error had probably just made her day.

Once things got quiet again, I reached for my cell phone. "Hey, Jake. What are you up to?"

"As a matter of fact, I'm making a pot of turkey chili," he said. My husband loved making chili, and using ground turkey and chicken instead of ground beef had become his new favorite substitution. I had to admit that it was quite good, but I did wish that he'd branch out and try to make something that *didn't* involve chili powder. "What's on your mind?"

"I had visits from our two main suspects this morning," I admitted, "and I don't quite know what to make of either one of them."

"Tell you what. I'll be there in three minutes, and you can tell me all about it."

I suddenly felt bad about interrupting his cooking. "You don't have to come over right away."

"No worries. The chili's already made. It just needs to rest and cool down before I put it away," he said.

I glanced at the clock. "Tell you what. I only have another forty-five minutes until I close," I said. "Why don't you wait until then, and we can chat while I clean up?"

"This isn't a ruse to get me over there to do dishes, is it?"

he asked me suspiciously. "I've already done them here, and my fingers are wrinkly as it is."

"I promise, all you have to do is hang out while I work," I said with a laugh.

"Are you sure it's nothing pressing that you want to discuss?" he asked me.

"If it were, I'd ask you to come right away. It's just that a few curious things have happened, but nothing even remotely dangerous."

"I don't know, Suzanne. One of those two women most likely killed Dusty Baxter, so I'd call *any* interaction with them potentially treacherous."

"I suppose so," I admitted. "I just have a hard time seeing either one of them as a killer."

"Does Max or Emily fit the bill more in your mind? I know we have reason to believe they are both innocent, but we could be wrong."

"It's happened before," I said as someone walked into the shop. "I've got to go."

"Is one of them there now?" Jake asked, his voice immediately tensing up.

"No, it's just Arnie White," I said.

"What's that supposed to mean?" Arnie asked as I ended the call with Jake.

"I was just talking to my husband," I said. "As a matter of fact, I've been looking for you."

Arnie looked at me suspiciously. "Why would you do that? I just came by for a cherry-filled donut and a cup of coffee."

"Answer one question for me and they're both on the house," I said as I got him his order.

"Gee, I don't know. I don't mind paying, you know."

"Suit yourself. That'll be twenty dollars," I said with a straight face.

"For a donut and a cup of coffee?" he protested loudly.

"Hey, you're the one who didn't want to answer my question," I said with a grin.

"Let's hear it," he said, resigned to playing my little game with me.

I had a hunch that he might. I could never have pulled a stunt like that if I'd been working for someone else, but that was the beauty of being my own boss.

Nobody could fire me.

"You were working on the newsstand when it flooded," I opened with.

"I was," he said happily as he reached for the treats.

"That wasn't the question. In fact, it was just a statement."

"Go on then, ask away." Arnie looked a little upset about not getting off so easily, but I couldn't afford to let him leave quite yet.

"You and Michelle Pennington were dating at the time," I said, "and before you acknowledge that fact as well, I still haven't come to my question yet." When he didn't answer, I asked, "Well?"

"I'm still waiting for the question," he said.

"What happened to the key you got from Emily Hargraves when you were finished with your work for her? That's my question."

"Are you sure I can't just pay you for this stuff?" he asked, looking uncomfortable.

"I'm sure. Why don't you want to tell me?"

"Because it sounds crazy," he said. After a few moments of thought, Arnie finally shrugged. "What could it possibly matter now?"

"That's what I want to know. Why are you so reluctant to tell me?"

"I think Michelle took it, okay? It was on my key ring, she

came over, and then it wasn't. I had to borrow Sam Winston's key to get into the shop one more time to finish the job."

"Did you ask her about it at the time?"

"You obviously don't know Michelle all that well. She had a temper then, and it's just gotten worse since we broke up, but she took it, all right. I'm sure of it."

That was more than I'd hoped to get out of him. I handed him the coffee and donut. "Thanks. Would you do me a favor and not mention this to Michelle or anyone else?"

"I was just about to ask you the exact same thing," he said. "Trust me, you don't want that woman mad at you. Take some free advice worth every penny it's costing you; steer clear of Michelle Pennington. She's got a bite worse than you can imagine."

Once Arnie was gone, I realized that I just had new and stronger reasons to suspect my final two suspects of murder. Hattie's disheveled appearance and odd behavior made her a real possibility in my mind, and Michelle's theft of the key gave her access to the stuffed animals, which had started this whole mess in the first place.

"There's got to be something we can do to flush the real killer out," I told Jake later as I had my arms buried in soap suds in the donut shop sink. Jake had pulled the stool over and was keeping me company as I worked cleaning up Donut Hearts. The truth was that it was nice having him there. I just wished his visit had been under more agreeable circumstances. I'd brought him up to date on what I'd discovered since we'd last chatted, and he'd taken it all in, mulling it all over as he nibbled on a sour cream cake donut.

"Suzanne, we need to think of a way to apply a little pressure and see if we can make one of them crack," he said after a few moments.

"I know you did that as a cop, but we can't exactly threaten either one of them," I said.

"Not with incarceration, but there are other inducements at our disposal."

"Withholding donuts from them doesn't have quite the same sting to it, does it?" I asked as I slid a few more dirty plates into the sudsy water. There were times when doing dishes by hand was therapeutic, but this didn't happen to be one of them. I was thoroughly tired of the process at the moment, but then again, it felt as though I was on my hundredth batch of dirty dishes for the day.

"Let's think about what we can come up with," he said. After he finished the donut he'd been snacking on, he asked, "Are there any more of those just lying around?"

"Sorry, that was the last one," I said. "Besides, I figured we could go grab a bite at the Boxcar before we started investigating again. That is if you're even hungry anymore."

"Try me," he said with a grin. "Making chili and thinking are both hard work, and I've done both of them this morning. I'd offer you some chili right now, but we both know it's better if it sits in the fridge for a day or two."

"Then we'll grab something to eat and see what we can come up with," I said. "I need five more minutes here, and we can be off. Can you hold off snacking on something else until then, or is there any danger that you're going to just waste away in the meantime?"

"I think I can make it," he said, tweaking my shoulder lightly.

It turned out that we weren't going to get a chance to have lunch in a timely manner after all, though. As we left the donut shop, me with the day's deposits tucked under my arm, someone started calling out my name from down the street. "Suzanne. Suzanne."

I turned to see the mayor rushing toward us. In fact, I'd mostly forgotten about him taking off after Michelle earlier. That was just how crazy my day had been.

"What's going on, Mr. Mayor?" I asked him as he approached us, nearly out of breath.

"Michelle. I followed her," he said, trying to recover.

"Take it easy, George," Jake said. "Catch your breath, and then you can tell us. We were just heading over to the Boxcar for an early lunch so we could discuss where we should go from here. Care to join us?"

"That's just it," the mayor said, finally getting his wind back. "It's Michelle."

"What about her?" I asked as a hint of dread crept into my thoughts.

"I'm afraid she's gone," the mayor said.

CHAPTER 20

"**M**ICHELLE DIED?" I SCREECHED OUT, not caring who heard me. How could that be? I'd just seen her that morning!

"No, not that I know of," George said. "I just meant that I lost her."

"You need to be a little clearer when you say things like that," I chided George.

"Sorry," he said with a shrug.

"What did you mean when you said that she was gone?" Jake asked him. "Do you know for a fact that she's left town, or is it that you just don't know where she is?"

"What I mean to say is that I can't find her," George admitted. "Sorry I'm not being easier to follow. I didn't get much sleep last night, and I can't go without it like I used to be able to."

"When was the last time you saw her?" I asked him. "I mean *after* you followed her from the donut shop."

"I trailed her all the way to work without any problem," George reported. "I figured she'd be there awhile, so I sat on a bench just down the street and watched as covertly as I could. From where I was sitting, I could keep an eye on her car *and* the front door of her office, so I figured I'd be safe."

"So what happened?" I asked him gently.

"The sun was warm, and I was a little bored waiting for her. I must have fallen asleep. When I woke up, her car was gone. I went by her apartment, but she wasn't there, either."

"Did you ask inside the accounting office?" Jake asked him.

"I was about to, but then I realized that I had no earthly reason to inquire about where she'd gone," George admitted. "The truth is that Harvey Bascomb is a big-time supporter of mine, and I can't really afford to have him wondering what I'm up to."

I was afraid of something exactly like that happening when I'd kept George at a distance during my previous investigations, but it certainly wasn't time to remind him of that. "Don't worry. We'll take care of it, George. You've been a big help."

"I don't see how," George lamented. "Maybe I'm too old to be doing this after all."

"Nonsense," Jake said, slapping the mayor hard on the back. "You dropped the ball, that's it, plain and simple. It could have happened to anyone."

"It's nice of you to say so, but I doubt that you would have fallen asleep on a stakeout," George said sadly.

Jake just shrugged, so I decided to step in. "George, we'll get to the bottom of this, and if we need any more help, you're the first person we'll call."

That seemed to brighten his mood a little. "Really? Do you mean that?"

"I do," I said. Right then and there I resolved to do just that if we needed a third person. At the moment though, what we really needed was to find out what Michelle was up to, and just as important, where she'd gone.

"Fine, then," George said. "Don't forget, if you need me, I'll be in my office."

"Sounds good," I said as I patted his shoulder.

After he left, I looked at Jake. "Have you ever fallen asleep on a stakeout?"

"Not yet, but the day is still fairly young," he said, trying to brush the question off. "I'm guessing my lunch is going to be delayed yet again, isn't it?"

"We can eat first if you have your heart set on it," I told him.

"No, business has to come before pleasure," he said as he noticed something in the bookstore window across the street.

As Jake started to walk over there, I tugged on his arm. "As much as I love to encourage you to read, we don't have time to browse at the bookstore right now."

He pointed to the window. "Trust me, we need to make this particular stop," he said, and then I saw what had caught his attention.

Apparently Paige was going to give us a perfect reason to go back to the accounting firm after all.

"Hey, I see you're selling raffle tickets," I told Paige as we walked in. I loved visiting the bookstore, walking the aisles of old favorites and new discoveries. April Springs had been really lucky when its owner had decided to come to town and open it. "What's the cause?"

"It's to provide books to kids who couldn't otherwise afford them. I'm a sucker for things like that," she said. "The tickets are five dollars apiece, and you have a chance to win a two-night stay at the Nascent Inn in the Smokies. It's supposed to be very posh. Would you like to buy one?"

"We can do better than that," I said. "How would you like it if we *sold* some for you?"

"Ordinarily I'd say that would be great, but why do I have the feeling that you two are up to something?" she asked us with a grin.

"Us? We're just trying to help out a good cause," I said,

pretending to be offended by the implication. I couldn't do it though, and I started grinning as well.

"You know what? I don't care *what* your motivation is," she answered as she handed over the booklet still filled with a great many tickets. "Have them hold onto their stubs and put their names and phone numbers on the tickets themselves."

"We can do that," I said with a smile. "Thanks."

"Thank *you*," she said. "Is there any chance this is tied into Dusty Baxter's murder?" Paige asked softly.

Jake just shrugged, but I said, "Yes," at the same time, so it kind of defeated the purpose of him responding at all. "I can't say anything more, though," I added a little too late.

"I understand completely," Paige said. "Once it's all over though, I'd love to hear what happened. I've been a big fan of mysteries all of my life."

"This is very real," Jake said. "It's best we all remember that."

His words were sobering, and Paige nodded in agreement. "Of course. Good luck."

"Thanks," I said, wondering if she meant selling tickets or finding Dusty's killer. Either way, we'd probably need it.

As Jake and I walked into the accountant's office, we saw that Michelle had indeed abandoned her post. In a trash can by the wall, someone had discarded the donut box she'd purchased from me earlier, though whether anyone had eaten any or not I couldn't say. I suddenly had to know, so I took two steps toward the trash can when one of the boss's doors opened.

"What are you doing here, Suzanne?"

It was Harvey Bascomb, and it appeared that I'd been caught dead to rights.

"I was just about to knock on your door," I said, doing my best to cover for my odd behavior. "Do you know where Michelle is, by any chance?"

"Is there a particular reason you'd like to know?" Harvey asked me a little pointedly.

"Raffle tickets," I said, fanning the pad in my hand. "She really wanted one." It was a bold lie that could be easily verified or denied later, but I'd worry about that when it happened.

"Frankly, I find that hard to believe," Harvey said.

"Maybe I got it wrong, but it's for a good cause, and I felt as though I had to at least try," I said.

"I suppose I could take one off your hands," he said as he reached for his wallet. "How much are they?"

"Five dollars each. It's a fundraiser for literacy, and the prize is a trip to the Nascent Inn in the Smokies. Just jot your name and number down on the ticket," I said as I took his money.

"I have no need of a trip," he said.

"You could always put Michelle's name and number down," I suggested. I was curious to see if he knew it by heart, though I didn't really suspect that he would.

"It hardly matters to me. Put yours down, if you'd like," Harvey said.

"The truth is, we'd really love to talk to Michelle," Jake said.

"As would I," he answered a little testily. "She was here twenty minutes, and then she suddenly told me that she needed to go home."

"Interesting," I said. "Did she happen to say why?"

Harvey looked embarrassed. "She claimed that she had a bad donut, and it made her sick," he said, almost as an apology. "Don't let it bother you. Everyone has a bad day at the office now and then."

I walked over to the box and retrieved it. "I don't," I said. There were eleven donuts inside, along with one that had been cut in half. Given what she'd told me in the past, I couldn't imagine that she'd eat even that much of one. "I suppose this is the one that she claimed made her sick," I said, and then I ate it before anyone could say a word. "I'm not at all concerned. I stand by my food."

"Maybe it was something else then," Harvey said quickly. "Now, if you'll excuse me, we're shorthanded today, so I've really got to get back to work."

I thought about taking the box with me, but I didn't really need any more donuts, especially ones that had been thrown away.

Out on the sidewalk, Jake said, "That was not the wisest thing you've ever done."

"Why do you say that? There was nothing wrong with that donut when it left my shop this morning," I said.

"True, but how do you know the killer didn't dose it with something bad after it left your hands?" Jake asked.

"Honestly, that thought never even occurred to me," I said, sobered by what I might have just inadvertently done to myself.

"I wouldn't worry about it if I were you. Chances are you'll be fine," Jake added lamely.

"Only time will tell, I guess," I said. "I just can't bring myself to believe that there was anything wrong with it."

"You're probably right," Jake replied. "Let's go by Michelle's apartment and see if she's really sick."

"George said he already checked for her there," I reminded Jake.

"I know, but it couldn't hurt to see that for ourselves."

"You're right. Jake, you haven't lost confidence in our mayor, have you?" I asked as we got into my Jeep and headed for Michelle's apartment. I knew it was a duplex across town, since

I'd looked it up as soon as I realized that she was one of our main suspects.

"No, it's not that. Anyone can make a mistake."

"Even you?" I asked him.

"Even me," he answered.

"Care to give me any examples?" I asked with a grin.

"If it's all the same to you, I think I'll pass," he replied.

To my surprise, Michelle's car was parked in front of her duplex after all. "There's no way George could have missed that."

"Maybe she was gone, but now she's back home," Jake said as he got out of the Jeep.

"Maybe," I said.

Jake paused at Michelle's car, frowned, and that was when I realized that it was still running. Reaching in through the open window, he shut the engine off and took the keys.

"What's going on, Jake?" I asked him.

"I have no idea, but I'm about to find out," he replied as he pocketed the car keys.

As we approached the duplex's front door, Jake started to knock.

As he did, I was surprised to see that it was already open a bit.

My husband's reaction was almost automatic as he reached into his ankle holster and pulled out his weapon. It was beginning to be a much too frequent occurrence, in my opinion.

At least he didn't try to get me to stay behind this time as he started to go inside to investigate.

CHAPTER 21

A S WE MOVED OUR WAY through the apartment and entered the back bedroom, it initially looked identical to the scene we'd stumbled across at Dusty's, minus the stuffed animals.

Michelle lay on the bed, and there was a growing bloodstain on her white blouse and her colorful wrap. This time though, the knife was lying on the floor.

"Michelle?" I asked as I raced toward her.

Jake was careful to search the room first, but I had to see if she was still alive.

"Suzanne? What are you doing here? Somebody tried to kill me," she said groggily.

At least she was still alive. "Are you okay?" I asked inanely.

"Of course I'm not okay! Didn't you just hear me? Somebody stabbed me!"

"Take it easy. I'm calling you an ambulance."

As I pulled my phone out to dial 9-1-1, Jake showed her a clean handkerchief. "I'm going to press this against the wound. It's going to hurt, but we need to stop the bleeding until the ambulance gets here."

"Just do it," she said, and as Jake applied pressure to the wound, she started screaming. "You're hurting me."

"I'm sorry, but it needs to be done," Jake answered with a calm and level voice.

"Why are you being so cold to me?" she asked as I completed the emergency call and hung back up.

"I'm just trying to take care of you, Michelle," Jake said calmly.

"Why aren't they here yet?" she asked plaintively thirty seconds later.

"While we're waiting, who exactly was it that stabbed you, Michelle?" I asked her. A part of me felt as though I was ambushing her, but if I didn't ask the question, and quickly, I'd never get the chance to find out.

"I don't know. I didn't see who it was," she said, "but I smelled some really hideous perfume as it was happening."

I knew in an instant who it was as Jake asked her incredulously, "You got stabbed in the shoulder and you didn't see who did it?" It was clear he was having trouble buying it.

"It all happened so fast! I was walking past the bathroom, and someone lashed out at me with a knife. I can't say for sure, but I think it was a woman," she said. "The next thing I knew, I was being shoved down on the bed from behind. If I hadn't jerked forward when I was being attacked, I might be dead right now, just like Dusty."

I was about to ask her about the perfume again when the front door slammed open.

"Where's the emergency?" an EMT called out.

"We're back here," Jake yelled.

One of the EMTs checked out the compress Jake had applied. "Nice job. You a cop?"

"I was once, a long time ago," he said.

The man nodded, and then he started to reach for the bloodied knife on the floor.

Jake touched his arm lightly. "You need to leave that right where it is."

"I thought you said that you *used* to be a cop," the guy protested.

"Shouldn't you be taking care of your patient?" Jake asked him pointedly.

The EMT took the hint. "Sure." He turned to his partner and said, "Let's get her on the stretcher."

"I can walk with a little help," she argued.

"Sorry. It's company policy," he replied.

"Just do as they ask," I told her.

"Will you lock the house up?" Michelle asked as they were carting her away.

"Don't worry about a thing on this end. We'll take care of it," I said.

"Aren't you coming with me?" Michelle called out as they wheeled her outside toward the waiting ambulance.

"Sorry, but we have to wait for the police," Jake said.

I wasn't sure if Michelle was going to say anything else when the ambulance door slammed shut.

"You got it too, didn't you?" Jake asked me.

"The hideous perfume she described her attacker wearing," I agreed.

"Hattie Moon," Jake replied. "I'm not sure what she's trying to cover up, but whatever it is, it must be really bad."

"There's nothing wrong with wanting to smell nice," I said in her defense, though I agreed with my husband a thousand percent when it came to Hattie. A little light application would have gone a long way when it came to her technique. "But I get your point."

"The question is why would Hattie want to stab Michelle?" I asked.

"I'm not sure, but it has to have something to do with Dusty Baxter's murder," Jake said. "That's just too big a coincidence to swallow."

"What is?" Chief Grant asked as he walked in. "Nobody touched that, did they?" he asked as he pointed to the weapon used in the attack.

"Just the killer," Jake said.

"Good. Thanks for securing the crime scene. How badly was Michelle injured?"

"It appeared to me that the attacker missed all of the vital spots," Jake answered. "Unless I miss my guess, she should be fine after she gets over the scare of it."

"If she ever manages to do that," the chief said. "Did she have any idea as to who attacked her?"

I wanted to keep it to myself, and I thought about doing just that for a split second before I realized that Jake wouldn't stand for it anyway, so I might as well get some credit for disclosing my suspicions. "We think it might have been Hattie Moon," I told him.

Jake nodded in approval, but the police chief just scowled. "I was afraid of that."

"Why do you say that?" Jake asked. "Do you know something we don't?"

"Yes, as a matter of fact, I do," the chief replied.

When he didn't explain himself, I asked, "Would you care to share any of that with us?"

He clearly debated it for a few seconds before finally replying. "Everyone else is going to know soon enough. We've been looking for Hattie for the past hour."

"Because?" Jake asked, letting his question float in the air.

"Because we now have reason to believe that she's the one who killed Dusty Baxter," the police chief replied sadly.

CHAPTER 22

"WHY WOULD YOU THINK THAT?" I asked him before Jake could manage to do it.

"I'm not really sure I should be sharing that information with you, no offense, Suzanne," the police chief said.

I was about to accept his answer when Jake startled us both by speaking up. "You know, we've gone above and beyond the call of duty as ordinary citizens keeping you informed as to what we know. Suzanne and I are not exactly without our own investigative abilities. Who knows? We might even be able to shed some light on something in a way that you haven't thought of yourself."

"You know something, Jake? Every day you're off the force, you sound more and more like a civilian," Chief Grant snapped at my husband. It was probably the biggest insult he could have made toward Jake, a decorated state police investigator who had served with distinction for many years, and what was more, it was clear that he immediately realized his blunder. "Strike that. I didn't mean it, and you know it. I'm just under a lot of pressure to solve Dusty's murder, and I haven't been getting much sleep lately anyway."

"It's fine," Jake said coolly, making it very clear that it was anything *but* fine with him. "We'll leave you to it, then. I'm sure you've got more important things to do than deal with a couple of *civilians*." He then turned to me and said, "Come on, Suzanne. I don't want to be *anywhere* that I'm not wanted."

"I'm right behind you," I said. I was getting ready to blast the police chief myself, but Jake put a hand on my shoulder and smiled softly, though the chief couldn't see it. What exactly was my cagey husband up to? As I walked past the chief, not only did I not say a word to him, I didn't even glance in his direction.

"Hang on a second," the chief said.

"Is that an order?" Jake asked as he stopped to look back at the young chief.

"I said I was sorry, okay? What more do you want from me?"

"Not a thing, sir. Not a thing."

Jake started walking again when the chief hurried to stop us from getting into my Jeep.

"You've never called me sir in my life," the chief said.

"You've never acted as though it was all that important to you," Jake replied.

Stephen Grant took less than a second to make a decision, one that I was fairly sure was going to go in our direction. "I found a bloody scarf," the chief said softly.

"You found what?" I asked him, clearly much louder than he would have liked.

In a soft voice, he said, "Suzanne, this isn't information I want the general public to have access to. Early this morning, we got an anonymous tip to look in Hattie's basket on her tricycle. It was parked out in front of the post office when I was driving past, so I had myself a peek."

"Did you search it illegally?" Jake asked.

"No, it's not like the thing even has a top on it. I looked at it from underneath, and through the wicker, I could see something that looked as though it might be significant. It had been initially wrapped in newspaper, but part of it had come undone, and I saw a bloodstained bit of fringe. I confiscated it and had some tests run, and guess what?"

"The blood belonged to Dusty Baxter," I said before he could answer.

"I wasn't really expecting you to guess, Suzanne," the chief said, looking a bit annoyed at me for jumping to the right conclusion, if I was in fact correct.

"But I'm right, aren't I?"

"You are," he said gently. "I need to have a long and serious chat with Hattie Moon, and I need to do it right now."

"Why would she kill Dusty, though?" I asked him. I wasn't at all sure how long this mutual cooperation was going to last, so I wanted to take full advantage of it while I could. "If he owed her money, she had to know that she'll never get it back now."

"I don't have to tell you how volatile Hattie Moon is," the chief said. "Are you really all that surprised she might stab him in the heart if he provoked her enough?"

I considered some of my past interactions with the woman, and I knew that the chief was right. Still, there were other loose ends that needed to be considered as well. "Are you saying that she stole Cow, Spots, and Moose as well? It seems like a lot to go through just to get back at Emily's boyfriend for not casting her for the lead in a silly little play."

"Does it really, though?" the chief asked.

"No, it makes perfect sense to me," Jake interjected. "I can see the crime of passion and even the stuffed animal abductions, but why go after Michelle and Max? Those are the bits I can't seem to understand."

For my husband to admit that was saying something. The chief just shrugged. "Maybe Michelle knows something, and she just doesn't realize it. Perhaps Hattie was going to try to frame her with evidence after Michelle was dead and she couldn't deny anything. As to Max, she could have decided she might as well take care of all of her enemies at one time. Who knows? I'll be sure to ask her the second I find her."

"May we tag along?" I asked, realizing that there was no way in the world he would ever agree to that, no matter how badly he wanted to get back into my husband's good graces. "We'll stay out of your way."

"Sorry, but I have to draw the line somewhere." He looked honestly upset that he had to refuse our request, though. Was there a loophole I wasn't seeing?

Evidently my husband knew what to say. "I know you can't sanction our presence officially," Jake said. "But what would happen if we went to see Hattie ourselves about an entirely unrelated matter, done purely by chance?"

The chief smiled a little before he wiped it quickly from his face. "I don't suppose there would be anything I could do about that."

"Well, we understand your position, so we won't ask to go with you again," Jake said.

The chief nodded, but it seemed to me that he was still feeling guilty about what he'd said to my husband, who had acted as mentor to him for a long time. Jake must have noticed it, too. He stood in front of the chief and put out his hand. "We're good."

The relief on Chief Grant's face was obvious, and I was glad yet again that I'd married such a kind and good man. "Thanks. I appreciate that."

"Don't mention it," Jake said, and then he turned to me and added, "Suzanne, do you feel like going for a little drive?"

"You bet I do," I said. It was all I could do not to tell the police chief that we'd see him at Hattie's, but that would have kind of ruined the little play that he and Jake had just performed for each other's benefit.

As I drove over to Hattie's just behind the police chief's squad car, I risked a glance over at my husband. "You're quite the rascal, aren't you?"

"What do you mean?" he asked as innocently as he could manage. It might have fooled a few folks, but it certainly wouldn't convince me.

"I saw you play the chief just then. Your feelings weren't really all that hurt by being called a civilian, were they?"

"It stung a little. I won't lie to you," he said.

I felt a bit more sympathy for my husband when he admitted to that. There was no doubt in my mind that he was being absolutely honest about it. "I'm sorry. Have I ruined you with my amateur sleuthing?"

"Suzanne, I wouldn't have missed what we've done for anything in the world."

"But you still miss being a cop, don't you? An investigator, I mean."

"Of course I do," he answered. "If you stopped making donuts tomorrow, don't you think you'd miss it?"

"Eventually, I suppose that I would," I said.

Jake just laughed. "Like in three or four hours? It's in your blood, just like being a cop was in mine."

"You could always go back, you know. I'm sure they would take you in a heartbeat." While I was my husband's biggest fan, I knew that there were rivals in the state police who would be thrilled to have Jake on the job again.

"I've thought about it," he said after a few moments.

This was news to me. "Really? It's okay, you know."

Jake took a moment, and then he reached over and patted my knee. "I appreciate that, but for right now, I'm enjoying being here with you. Is that okay?"

"That's fine and dandy with me, sir. In fact, it's terrific!" We drove a few more minutes when I said, "Still, you weren't nearly as hurt as you pretended to be."

"Is there a question in there somewhere?" he asked with a slight smile.

"No, it's simply a statement of fact."

Jake held it in for a few moments, and then he laughed loudly. "I was about to say something stinging in reply when I thought, what would Suzanne do?"

"Wow, I'm honored. So, what did you come up with?"

"I thought about how I could use the perceived slight to help our investigation," he admitted. "How did I do?"

"It's scary to me how good you were," I admitted. "Do you think Hattie did everything the chief said she did?"

"I honestly don't know," Jake said after a few moments. "When you look at it one way, it certainly adds up. Then again, we may all be off base. Either way though, I'd love the chance to speak with her."

"Well, it appears that you're in luck," I said as I pulled into Hattie's place behind the chief. The infamous tricycle was parked haphazardly in the front yard, but that wasn't the main thing that held my attention.

Millie Farnsworth rushed up to the chief's patrol car before he had time to come to a complete stop. The poor woman looked as though she was about to have a stroke, and I had to wonder what news she was about to share with the police, and by extension, the two of us.

CHAPTER 23

"SHE'S NOT HERE!" MILLIE SAID, her words rushing out of her in a flood.

"Her tricycle is right there," I said calmly. "Everyone knows that she doesn't go *anywhere* without it. Take a deep breath, Millie, and try to calm down."

"I can't," she said as she began to pace. "I happened to be looking out my back window at my bird feeder. The squirrels keep getting into it, and I don't know what to do. I've tried everything." The woman was absolutely babbling now.

"I've got some ideas I can share with you later," I said, "but you were telling us about Hattie."

"That's right. I'm sorry. I don't know what I'm doing."

When she paused for a moment longer, the chief said, "You were watching the squirrels in your feeder, and you saw something. What did you see?"

"Hattie had a suitcase in her hand, and she was running out into the woods behind us. Hattie hates the woods! And she'd never go *anywhere* she couldn't get on her tricycle. Something is terribly wrong. She'd never just leave it like that!" Millie pointed to the trike to emphasize her point.

"Take it easy, Millie," the chief said in a reassuring voice. "Why don't you go back inside, and we'll see if we can't find out what's going on?"

"I couldn't bear to be shut out of this," she said, wringing her hands together. "I'm worried sick about Hattie. The fact is that she's been acting odd ever since Dusty was murdered."

That got Jake's attention. For a moment he forgot that he wasn't the one running the investigation. "How exactly do you mean?"

"She's been paranoid, peeking out behind her curtains, coming in at the oddest times, and worst of all, she's been avoiding me. She looks absolutely guilty about something, or terrified. I have no idea which it is. She's not herself at all."

"We'll find out what's going on," he said. "Suzanne, why don't you take Millie inside and make her a cup of tea?"

Was he really trying to get rid of me that easily? I wasn't going to do it! There was no way I was going to allow them to investigate Hattie's place without me, and I was about to protest when Millie said, "What I really need to do is lie down. I feel the need to take to my bed."

It was an expression I hadn't heard in donkey years, but I wasn't about to let the opportunity it presented slip through my fingers. "That's exactly what you should do then. Go rest, Millie. You deserve it. You're a good friend to Hattie, and I know that she appreciates you."

I had no idea if she was all that good a friend or not, but I wanted to ease the woman's mind. "Thank you, Suzanne. Goodness knows I try."

Once she was inside her house, I turned to the chief. "Nice try."

"I thought she could use the company."

"It appears she's fine without any," I said. "Now, shall we go check on Hattie's place and see if we can find anything that might tell us what she's up to?"

"I'm not so sure you should come in with me, even if the door is open, which it probably isn't."

Jake said, "Suzanne could be really useful, Chief. Maybe

she'll spot something that we could easily miss. A woman's perspective could be helpful."

I wasn't sure if I liked the way the conversation was headed, but if it would get me inside the house with them, I was all for it.

The chief simply shrugged as he approached the door.

He didn't invite us to follow him, but then again, he didn't expressly forbid it, so my husband and I both chose to take it as a sign that he was okay with our presence.

Unfortunately, the door was locked, so maybe it would be a moot point after all.

"Millie said that Hattie ran away from the back of the house. Could *that* door be unlocked?" I asked.

"I'm not sure, but it's worth a try," Jake said.

We waited and let the chief lead the way. After all, it was technically his investigation at that point, not ours.

The door was blessedly unlocked.

Not only that, it was standing wide open.

The chief drew his weapon, and Jake followed suit.

"Nobody's home, guys. Remember?" I reminded them.

"It never hurts to play it safe," Jake said, and the chief nodded in agreement.

"Stay behind us," he instructed me.

I had no problem with that. As we went from room to room in the small cottage, I realized that Hattie wasn't much of a housekeeper, or else something very wrong was going on. The place was a wreck, so much so that I couldn't be sure if she'd been robbed recently or she was just a slob. When we got to her bedroom, the last room on our list, we found it devoid of life as well, just as Millie had said. At least there weren't any bodies there. I counted my blessings for that. I went into the master bathroom and came back out again in a few seconds. After checking a few dresser drawers and her closet, I turned to the men and said, "She's clearly planning on staying away awhile."

"How can you possibly know that?" the chief asked.

"Her makeup kit is gone, along with her toiletries and enough clothes to last her two weeks based on the empty spaces in her dresser. If I know Hattie, she headed out with the thought that she wasn't coming back anytime soon."

"Don't worry. We'll find her," the chief said.

"Do you really think she killed Dusty?" I asked him.

"Why else would she shoot at Max, attack Michelle, and then run away? If you ask me, we've got our killer."

The chief of police sounded so sure that I felt a little relief from the fact that I wouldn't have to keep jumping at shadows.

"So, what do we do now?" Jake asked him.

"I can't imagine her getting too far on foot. I'm heading into the woods to see if I can find her."

"Want some company?" Jake volunteered.

The chief didn't even hesitate. "I'll call some backup for us, but that would be great." He then turned to me and added, "Suzanne, I'm sorry, but you can't come with us."

"That's fine with me," I said. "I want to go by and check on Michelle, anyway."

"You don't have to do that," the chief said.

"I know, but I feel a little guilty suspecting her of murder," I admitted. I turned to my husband and asked, "Are you going to be okay, Jake?"

"I've never been better," he said, and I realized that it was true.

"Don't take any unnecessary risks," I told him.

"I'll be as careful as I can," he told me with a grin.

"Hey, Penny. Could you tell me what room Michelle Pennington is in?" I asked my nursing friend at the hospital.

"Hi, Suzanne. She's in 227."

"How's she doing?"

"The rules and regulations don't allow me to share that kind of patient information with non–family members," she said as she winked at me and gave me a thumbs-up. "I hope you understand."

"Completely," I said with a smile.

"We have a staff meeting about to start, so we're a little shorthanded at the moment, but she's just down the hall if you want to pop in on her."

I found Michelle in a room by herself. Her section of the hospital was curiously empty of patients, and it was a bit eerie not having the buzzing of activity around her. She was lying in bed staring out the window when she realized I was there.

"Hello, Suzanne. What brings you here?"

"I wanted to check up on you," I said. "I'm sorry if I've been a little rough on you lately. How's your shoulder?"

"The doctors say that I was lucky. From the angle I was stabbed, it ended up being a shallow wound. Do the police have any idea who attacked me?"

"It appears that it was Hattie Moon," I said, watching her reaction.

She looked shocked by the suggestion, but I couldn't tell if it had been rehearsed or not. "Hattie? I was afraid of that."

"Why do you say that?" I asked her as I took a seat by her bed.

"A few minutes ago, I remembered where I'd smelled that perfume. It had to be Hattie, or another woman with equally bad taste in fragrances."

"Why would she attack you, though?" I asked her.

"I saw her at Dusty's place a few days ago," she said. "She

looked startled being caught there, and I wondered what she'd been up to."

"Evidently Dusty owed her money," I said.

"I knew all about that. This was different. Her lipstick was smudged a little, and when I walked in, I asked Dusty about it. Apparently Hattie tried to pressure him into doing something he didn't want to do, and when he rejected her, she was furious about it. She had to know that Dusty would tell me all about it."

"Did you tell the police any of this?" I asked her as I leaned forward.

"I meant to, but what with everything that was going on, I never got a chance to. The truth is, I didn't want to embarrass Hattie, but after she tried to kill me, I'm a lot less reluctant to turn her in."

"She's on the run right now," I told her. "The police are actively searching for her."

"I just hope they don't believe her lies. The woman's an actress. There's no doubt in my mind that she'll deny everything."

I was about to tell her that they had evidence when she complained, "Suzanne, I need my lip balm. Would you grab it for me? They put my clothes in the closet."

I did as she asked, and as I opened the door to retrieve it, I asked her, "Where's your wrap?" She'd been wearing one when we'd found her, which hadn't really surprised me all that much.

"I had to throw it out. It was ruined in the attack. What a pity. It was one of my favorites."

The woman did love her clothing accessories.

But I suddenly realized that Hattie didn't.

In fact, in all of the years I'd known her, I'd never seen her wear a wrap, a pashmina, a stole, or anything like it.

And I'd never, ever seen her wear a scarf.

Michelle, on the other hand, was rarely without one.

So how had Hattie worn one on the day of the murder and never any other time?

The truth hit me like a fist.

She hadn't.

The real killer had to be lying in bed three steps from me.

I started for the door when I heard her say, "Suzanne, I really need that lip balm."

"I'm sorry. I just remembered something," I said as I took a step toward freedom so I could get help.

With a swiftness that shocked me, Michelle leapt from the bed and launched herself toward me before I could even cry out.

I could have handled her if we'd both been unarmed, but then I saw a glint in the light coming from a sharp surgical scalpel in her hand, and I realized that it was pointed straight at my throat.

"Not a word out of you or you're dead meat," she said as she motioned me back to my chair.

I could have screamed then, but I knew if I did, it would be the last sound I ever uttered.

Dutifully, I did as she instructed.

How on earth was I going to get myself out of this jam?

CHAPTER 24

"DON'T DO IT," I PLED with her, hoping that somehow I could turn the tables on this killer, or that someone would come in and save me.

"Why shouldn't I?" she asked with a mad laugh. "If I was willing to stab myself in the shoulder, why shouldn't I kill you? After all, they can't hang me twice."

"Why *did* you kill Dusty?" I asked. "Don't you want someone to know? Besides, who am I going to tell?"

"What could it hurt at this point? He dumped me for Emily Hargraves," she said, spitting the words. "The sick thing was she didn't even want him! When she spurned him, he let himself into her shop with my key and stole her stuffed animals. It was his ploy to be the hero and get them back for her. He even wrote a juvenile ransom note to throw everyone off. Dusty thought it might just change her mind about him."

It might even have worked, especially if Max hadn't been in the picture. Emily loved those stuffed animals more than any reasonable person could understand, and it impressed me that Dusty had gotten it, even if I didn't approve of his tactics.

"I bet that crushed you," I said, trying my best to sound sympathetic as I kept glancing at the door. If the staff hadn't been in a meeting, if the police hadn't been focused on Hattie, if a thousand other things had happened, I might stand a chance, but it didn't feel as though there was going to be any help for me on this one.

I was going to have to overpower her myself, but my tools to fight back were limited. If I could keep her talking, though, I might still have a chance of making it out alive.

"I went to his place and told him I loved him," she said, frowning as she told her story. "He laughed at me, and then he led me to his bedroom where he had the stuffed animals all set up. He told me his plan, and then he said that even if it didn't work, he was finished with me. He told me that I was used up! I grabbed a knife from the dresser, and before I knew what was happening, I stabbed him with it! You should have seen the shocked expression on his face! He couldn't believe it was happening. He clawed at the knife, and then he grabbed me and pulled me to him. As the knife clattered to the floor, he managed to get blood all over my scarf! Once he was dead, I realized what I'd done, but I couldn't just confess and go to jail! I threw the knife onto one of the cows and I left."

"Taking your bloody scarf with you," I said. "Why did you keep it, though? Wasn't it too incriminating for you to have in your possession?"

"I thought it might be useful," she said. The woman was a true schemer; that was certain. "It was, too."

"So you decided to plant it in Hattie's basket and then call the police with a hot tip," I said.

"I thought it would get her locked up, but it ended up being what gave me away, wasn't it?" She seemed particularly curious, and I decided to indulge her. After all, at least it would buy me some time. The only thing I had within reach was a hospital pillow and sheet, neither one of them much use against sharp steel.

"You always dress so stylishly with scarves, pashminas, and wraps, and I suddenly realized that I'd never seen Hattie wearing one," I confessed.

"A man would have missed that," she said. "Fortunately,

you're the only woman who knows me and is involved in the case. I might just get away with this after all."

"How are you going to explain my death?" I asked, choking on my own words.

"You said it yourself. Hattie is on the run. Clearly she stormed in here, and she did it. I may have to knock myself unconscious, but it will be worth it."

"Jake won't buy it," I said.

"Wait until he hears my spin on it," she answered.

"Why set Hattie up, though? Why not Emily? Or Max? Were you the one who took a shot at Max at the lake?"

"I was just shooting randomly at the cabin. I knew you and your husband were investigating the murder, and I wanted to scare you off. Was that really Max in the doorway? I thought it was Jake. Anyway, I'm glad that he's okay. I had considered framing him or Emily, but then I overheard a cop saying that they were both in the clear. I had no choice but to go after Hattie, but every time I tried to plant that bloody scarf, her nosy neighbor was watching. She should be next, after I finish with you. Sorry, Suzanne, but your time is up."

Michelle must have been working up her nerve to kill me in cold blood.

Evidently, she was ready.

Unfortunately for her, though, so was I.

CHAPTER 25

As she lunged for me, I did the only thing I could think to do.

I grabbed the pillow and swung it at the knife with all that I had.

It didn't knock it out of her hand. In fact, it didn't even come close, but it did manage to startle her.

I pushed Michelle aside, knocking her down in my eagerness to escape, and I raced for the door, hoping that someone would be nearby to help me with this killer.

I didn't make it, though.

Suddenly, a hand grabbed my ankle, and before I knew what was happening, I was being pulled down to the floor beside her.

In her anger at being attacked, she must have forgotten about the knife momentarily, but when I looked over at her, I saw that she was doing her best to recover it to finish me off.

I couldn't let that happen, though.

I reached the knife a split second after her hand wrapped around it, but that didn't mean that she'd won. Instead of going for the weapon, I grabbed the hand holding it.

"Stop being so difficult," she panted as she fought for control.

My only answer was a war scream that shook the walls. If I was going to die anyway, at least she wasn't going to get away with it.

The sound shocked her. "Shut up!" Her scream was nearly as loud as mine.

As hard as she tried, Michelle didn't manage to break my grip, but she caught me off guard, and in a surprise twisting move, she jammed the knife toward my throat.

I somehow managed to deflect it, but as I did, she snapped her wrist again, and the blade pierced my arm.

At first I didn't feel its sting, but then, as I looked down and saw the blood, I felt a wave of pain and nausea sweep over me.

Not only had she wounded me, but the blood was making my grip on her hand slippery! If I let up for one second, I knew that I was dead.

Trying to beat back the pain, I kept fighting for control of the knife. Every ounce of my being was focused on wrestling it from Michelle's grip.

But I knew that I was losing the battle.

If no one came to my rescue soon, I realized that I wasn't going to win this final battle.

I wasn't going to die without a fight, though. If Michelle managed to kill me, it wouldn't be without me fighting back with every last ounce of energy I possessed.

I was a moment from being overcome when I heard a joyous sound.

The hospital room door opened.

Someone had heard my scream after all!

The only problem was that Michelle had somehow managed to finally break free from my grasp.

I looked to see her drawing the knife back to strike a deadly blow to my heart, just as she had done to Dusty Baxter, and I took what I realized might be my last breath on earth.

"Don't do it," George Morris said as he held his handgun pointed straight at Michelle.

"You don't have the guts to shoot me," Michelle said, but I noticed that the knife drooped a little in her hands as she said it.

"Try me," George said. Without even looking at me, he asked, "Suzanne, are you okay?"

"I'm fine," I said.

"What's that blood doing on your arm, then?" he asked.

"I'm not saying I'm perfect," I said, fighting the urge to giggle, scream, or maybe even pass out. It seemed to take all of my energy just to focus on what was happening.

"Okay then," he said. "Michelle, this is your last chance."

I could hear footsteps running down the hallway toward us now. Michelle wasn't going to talk her way out of this one, and she knew it.

To my surprise, and to George's as well, she reversed the course of her knife at the last second and plunged it toward her own chest, trying to cheat us from catching her after all.

Unfortunately for Michelle, her aim wasn't as true as it had been with Dusty, and there was a crack team of doctors and nurses steps away to save her from her own folly.

Apparently Michelle was going to have to face charges for what she'd done, and I was going to do everything in my power to nail her hide to the wall.

After all, she'd almost been the end of me, and while I was a forgiving person by nature, that was a little beyond the scope of my understanding.

CHAPTER 26

A S I WAS GETTING STITCHES in my arm, I asked George, "What made you come by the hospital, anyway?"

"I'd love to say that I figured it out, but I was actually visiting someone on the other end of the floor when I heard your scream. You've got some lungs on you, woman."

"Thanks," I said. I was a little shaky at the moment, which was often the case when I'd had a brush with oblivion. I was ordinarily calm enough during a direct confrontation, even with a killer.

It was only afterward that I fell apart. "Where's Jake?"

"He's on his way," the mayor said.

"Would you have really shot her?" I asked George as the doctor finished up with me.

"I would have done it in a heartbeat," the mayor said, and I had no reason to doubt him.

"I'm glad you didn't have to," I answered, "but I appreciate you being willing to do it."

He touched my good shoulder lightly. "For you, I'd do anything, my friend."

It was as touching a moment as we'd ever had, and I was about to tear up when my mother came rushing in.

"I just heard the news," she said, her face white with fear. "Suzanne, are you all right?"

"I'm fine now, Momma. George here saved me."

"I did no such thing," the mayor protested even as my mother wrapped him in her embrace. It was a sight to see, given that she was nearly a foot shorter than he was, but I respected the effort. I would have hugged him myself if I could have.

"I don't believe you for a second," Momma said, kissed his cheek soundly, and then she turned back to me. "Suzanne, is there anything I can do for you? Anything at all?"

"Anything?" I asked.

"All you have to do is name it," she said.

"Well, I've got a dozen raffle tickets for literacy in my Jeep that I promised Paige I'd sell for her. Would you be interested in buying a few?"

Momma laughed long and hard, no doubt from relief as much as anything else. "I'll take them all," she said. "I'm so glad you're okay."

"That makes two of us," I said.

As I sat there patiently listening to Momma and George talk, I couldn't wait to see my husband. Being in Jake's arms right now was the *only* thing I needed, and I knew that it would do me more good than anything the modern medical community could ever provide.

Love mattered.

After all, Michelle had murdered Dusty because he had rejected her.

I had so much more in my life than she ever had.

Jake loved me, plain and simple, and it was something as important to me as oxygen.

And in the end, that was really all that mattered to me.

RECIPES

Apple Cinnamon Drops

One of my favorite ways of making donuts when I'm pinched for time is by whipping up a quick batter and then dropping balls of it straight into hot oil! There are no fussy proof times to worry about with these tasty little goodies. In a world full of instant gratification, these delightful little treats really fit the bill!

We recently started adding diced chunks of apples to the mix, much like Suzanne does in the book, and I must say, the results are excellent. You can play with different apple varieties, but in my opinion, you can't go wrong with Granny Smith apples.

Ingredients

Mixed
- 1 egg, lightly beaten
- 1/2 to 2/3 cup whole milk (the richer the better, but 2% or even 1% will do in a pinch) (you want a batter, not a dough, so add enough milk to attain that consistency)
- 1/3 cup sugar, white granulated
- 1/8 cup oil (canola is my favorite)

Sifted
- 1 cup flour, unbleached all-purpose (though bread flour will work as well)

- 2 teaspoons baking powder
- 1 and 1/2 teaspoons cinnamon
- 1 teaspoon nutmeg
- 1/4 teaspoon salt

Last-Minute Addition
- 1 diced apple, peeled (I prefer Granny Smith, but feel free to experiment)
- 1 teaspoon cinnamon
- canola oil, enough for frying (the amount depends on your pot or fryer)

Directions

Heat the oil (I like canola) to 365 degrees F.

In a medium-sized bowl, beat the egg thoroughly, and then add the milk, sugar, and canola oil, mixing well. Grab another bowl and sift together the flour, baking powder, cinnamon, nutmeg, and salt. Add the dry ingredients to the wet, mixing well until you have a smooth consistency. Finally, dice the apple and coat it with cinnamon. Then stir these bits into the batter and you're ready to fry!

Drop bits of batter using two tablespoons, one to scoop the batter and the other to peel it off into the oil. Fry for 1 1/2 to 2 minutes, turning halfway through, drain and then dust with confectioner's sugar.

Yield 12 to 16 donut drops

Spectacular Sour Cream Donuts

I have really grown to love a good sour cream donut, and this recipe tastes delightful. I usually ice these with a simple mix of confectioner's sugar and water, but they are good without any embellishments whatsoever, which is the true test of a donut, in my opinion. We're not coffee drinkers, but we enjoy these donuts with a cup of hot cocoa, no matter what time of year it might be!

Ingredients

Liquid
- 1 egg, beaten
- 1/2 cup sugar
- 1/4 cup buttermilk
- 1/4 cup sour cream
- 1 teaspoon vanilla

Dry
- 2 cups unbleached all-purpose flour
- 1 teaspoon baking powder
- 1/2 teaspoon baking soda
- 1/2 teaspoon nutmeg
- Dash of salt

Directions

Heat enough oil (I like canola) in a large pot to fry your donuts. I like to hit around 365 degrees F.

While you're waiting for the oil to come to temperature, take a medium-sized mixing bowl and beat the egg, then add the sugar, buttermilk, sour cream, and vanilla. Mix it all together thoroughly, and then set it aside.

In a separate bowl, sift the flour, baking powder, baking soda, nutmeg, and salt together, and then add the dry mix to the wet in thirds until it is all combined.

Roll the dough out to about 1/4 inch thick, then cut it into rounds and holes. If you don't have a cutter, use two different-sized drinking glasses.

Fry the donuts in the hot oil for 3 minutes, turning halfway through, then place them on paper towels to drain.

Powdered sugar can be applied immediately, but wait until they cool to add icing and sprinkles.

Makes 6 to 8 donuts and holes

Super Easy Fried Cherry Pies

We make these with just about any pie filling you might find on your grocer's shelves. While these will never be confused with gourmet treats, they are quite delicious, and I've never had any complaints! One of the best things about these is the fact that they look and taste as though they were a great deal more work than they really are!

Ingredients

- Cherry pie filling, 8 oz., from the can (or any other pie filling you might prefer)
- 1 tablespoon sugar, plain granulated
- 1 ready-made pie crust

Directions

This couldn't be easier. Simply unroll the pie crust onto your lightly floured countertop. Flour the rim of a drinking glass and cut circles out of the dough by pressing down and twisting. You can get four decent-sized fried pies out of one crust if you choose the size carefully. Place a small amount of filling in the center of each circle, wet the edges of the dough, and fold each circle in half. Use a fork to score the edges of the dough in place, making any design you wish, but making sure you get a seal all the way around the joined edges.

Drop the pies into the oil, allowing them to brown on each side, anywhere from 6 to 9 minutes total in my experience.

Scoop them out of the oil with a spatula or spider strainer, drain them on paper towels, and then dust them with powdered sugar. Let them cool a bit before you eat them, since they come out extremely hot!

Makes approximately 4 pies

If you enjoy Jessica Beck Mysteries and you would like to be notified when the next book is being released, please visit our website at jessicabeckmysteries.net for valuable information about Jessica's books, and sign up for her new-releases-only mail blast.

Your email address will not be shared, sold, bartered, traded, broadcast, or disclosed in any way. There will be no spam from us, just a friendly reminder when the latest book is being released, and of course, you can drop out at any time.

OTHER BOOKS BY JESSICA BECK

A Killer Cake
A Baked Ham
A Bad Egg
A Real Pickle
A Burned Biscuit

The Ghost Cat Cozy Mysteries
Ghost Cat: Midnight Paws
Ghost Cat 2: Bid for Midnight

The Cast Iron Cooking Mysteries
Cast Iron Will
Cast Iron Conviction
Cast Iron Alibi
Cast Iron Motive
Cast Iron Suspicion

Made in the USA
Columbia, SC
16 May 2020

97588071R00113